Skeleton in the Art Closet

A WATERCOLOR MYSTERY

To Kim,
I hope you'll enjoy

Gail Langer Karwoski

the crimes that darken
our art center!

Gail Karwoski
2023

Black Rose Writing | Texas

First printing

This is a work of fiction. Names, characters, businesses, places, events, and incidents are
either the products of the author's imagination or used in a fictitious manner. Any
resemblance to actual persons, living or dead, or actual events is purely coincidental.

ISBN: 978-1-68513-150-0
Library of Congress: 2022917490
PUBLISHED BY BLACK ROSE WRITING
www.blackrosewriting.com

Printed in the United States of America
Suggested Retail Price (SRP) $19.95

Skeleton in the Art Closet is printed in EB Garamond

*As a planet-friendly publisher, Black Rose Writing does its best to eliminate unnecessary waste to
reduce paper usage and energy costs, while never compromising the reading experience. As a result,
the final word count vs. page count may not meet common expectations.

Don't miss the first book of the
WATERCOLOR MYSTERY SERIES

A Brush with Murder

Gail Langer Karwoski

A WATERCOLOR MYSTERY

Praise for
Skeleton in the Art Closet

"Grab a cup of chamomile tea and curl up with Gail Langer Karwoski's follow-up mystery, featuring the cozy crew from Atkinsville. This time, the ladies grapple with a murder closer to home. Grab your book club besties and get lassoed into a fun new adventure with these artsy sleuths who remain the best of friends while figuring out whodunnit."

–Kim Siegelson, author of *Honey Bea*

"Something's afoot at the Atkinsville Arts Center! Jane Roland and her delightful Tuesday painting group ladies are back, searching for clues and discovering skeletons in the closet. A murder mystery full of twists and turns—and a buddy story full of enchanting personalities—will keep readers eagerly turning the page for the next brush stroke and clue."

–Bonnie Roberts, playwright of *The Enchanted April*

"*Skeleton in the Art Closet* has all the things I love in a cozy read: older female sleuths solving a mystery from the past, pets, baked goods, and art-loving folk solving mysteries via mimosas by the pool."

–J. Ivanel Johnson, author of *Just a Still Life*

For Janet Rodekohr,
talented painter, editor, and friend.

Skeleton in the Art Closet

CHAPTER ONE

While ladling ice from the punch bowl into a glass cup, Jane Roland heard the first scream.

She froze. A scream? Surely her ears had misinterpreted the sound.

Her nerves thawing, Jane picked up the ladle and splashed spiked cider over the ice in the cup. The second scream stopped her mid-splash. This scream was louder and more piercing than the first. Jane put down the cup, lest she drop it.

The third - louder still - was followed by a crescendo of insistent screams which seemed to gain intensity with repetition. The screams were coming from the direction of the Central Gallery.

All of the ordinary noises of an opening night reception at an art gallery - people greeting, laughing, feet shuffling, fabric swishing, glasses tinkling - disappeared. The crowd, with Jane among them, moved as if compelled by a magnetic force. They pushed through the doorway that led out of the Small Gallery toward the source of the screams.

In the larger gallery, the sound was panic personified. Horrifying screams bounced off the brick walls, the plaster ceiling, the polished wood floors. Terror penetrated deep inside Jane's brain and electrified her every nerve, forehead to toes. She stood on tiptoe and strained to locate the source of the sound, but she was a petite woman in a bulging crowd. Grey hairs and balding heads, dangly earrings, sport-coated shoulders, and silken scarves blocked her view.

At last, the screaming dissolved into weeping. Great gasping sobs. And a woman's soothing voice: "No, no, it's not real, Noah. Just a decoration. Because it's Halloween. That's all."

Another scream, this one assuming the shape of words. A child's trembling voice. "Yes, yes, it is. Look. See inside the bones. That grey bumpy stuff. That's marrow inside the bones. So, it IS real. It's from a dead body!"

Jane forced herself, wriggling and pushing, through the mass of bodies and into the eye of the storm. "It's not real," she announced to the small blonde boy gaping at the skeleton that dangled from the ceiling. Jane guessed he was about 6 years old. "I promise you, it's not real. I hung it up yesterday when we were decorating the gallery for the show. It's just a decoration." Turning to the woman kneeling beside the boy, Jane added. "I'm so sorry this scared him."

Jane stood on tiptoe and reached up to touch one of the skeleton's foot bones. She twisted the foot up and down, then looked at the child. "See how light the bones are? They're plastic. There's no marrow inside - just rough plastic with some dirt on it. Do you want me to pick you up so you can touch the bones?" Looking at the woman, Jane said, "His name is Noah? You're his mom?"

The mother nodded.

"It's a pretend skeleton, Noah," Jane continued her explanation, her voice high and shrill with tension. "I found it in the drawing classroom. Artists use this to sketch from. The bones are wired together. See? So the artists can pose the body and draw people in different positions; sitting down, reaching out, stepping forward."

As she babbled, Jane felt a hand on her shoulder. She was relieved to see Ruth Alice Morton, the Director of the art center.

"I had no idea something like this would happen," Jane said to Ruth Alice. "When I saw the skeleton in the drawing classroom, I thought it would be a nice touch. You know, Halloween theme, and this reception on Halloween weekend." Jane grimaced. "It just seemed like a good idea. To me, at least. I admit Chandler was hesitant." Chandler was the show curator. "But he humored me since it was my first time hanging a show. Maybe we should take it down? I don't want it scaring anybody else."

Ruth Alice smiled; a large, sunny smile that came from her whole body and communicated happiness. When Ruth Alice smiled, her brown cheeks, her round shoulders, even her purple-spotted eyeglasses seemed to radiate love and joy. It was one of the reasons - one of the many reasons - that both the artists and the volunteers at the Atkinsville Art Center (the AAC or "Ack" as everyone pronounced the acronym) adored this new director. Of course, part of Ruth Alice's appeal came from following a bad act. The last director had practically eviscerated the center. The treasury had dwindled to practically nothing, not to mention membership and attendance. And, as if that wasn't bad enough, the former director had just taken off. One fine day, he disappeared - into thin air.

"If you want to make AAC inviting for children, this is not the way to do it," said Noah's mother as she stood and dusted off the back of her dress.

Ruth Alice got down on one knee in front of the child so she could talk with him, eye to eye. "Do you think we should take down the skeleton, Noah?"

Noah nodded between sniffles.

"Okay, that's what we'll do. First thing tomorrow. Thank you for helping us decide which decorations to use, Noah. We have several schools scheduled to come see this show, and we wouldn't want to frighten any of the kids coming through the gallery, would we?"

Noah nodded again, still sniffling.

Ruth Alice gently took one of Noah's hands. "Art is for everybody, Noah. It makes the world a happier place. Nobody meant to scare you. Jane, here, she was kind enough to help Chandler hang the show. It took them days and days to get all these beautiful pictures hung on the walls. They weren't thinking the skeleton might be scary. Sometimes even grownups make mistakes. And mistakes are how we learn. You know?"

Noah nodded again. This time, he forced a tiny smile. His mother mouthed "thank you" to Ruth Alice and guided the boy away from the skeleton.

"We have some chocolate chip cookies on the refreshment table. Homemade," Ruth Alice called after them. Noah's mother smiled back.

"Well, that was a bit alarming," Ruth Alice said. She exhaled. "Never a dull moment."

"I'm sorry," Jane said. "It never even crossed my mind that the skeleton would scare someone. They're so common this time of year. Do you want me to come and take it down in the morning? I don't think I should bring in the ladder now, with everybody here."

"Don't worry about it," Ruth Alice said. "Chandler is working tomorrow afternoon. I'll get him to help me take it down."

"I don't want you and Chandler to waste your time taking it down. I feel like this is all my fault," Jane said. "It was my idea. Chandler told me he was afraid the skeleton would distract from the art."

"You should have listened to Chandler," a woman said. "Those screams were quite the distraction. I almost passed out."

Two members of Jane's Tuesday watercolor group, Donna Norton and Pam Gerald, had joined them. They stood, punch glasses in hands and smirks on lips.

Donna, her white hair topped with a black and orange beret, began to chuckle. Donna was the oldest member of their group, and she experienced fainting spells because of her high blood pressure. Jane usually found Donna's gruff, "heh, heh, heh," amusing. But right now, she was too tense to laugh.

"You know how I generally pass out whenever I see a dead body?" Donna added, looking at Ruth Alice, Jane, and Pam.

Pam grinned, "Nah, I wasn't worried. If I recall, you only pass out when the dead body is floating in water."

Donna and Pam were referring to their spring adventure at an art retreat, where four members of their group had gotten immersed in a real-life murder mystery involving dead bodies and bodies of water. Jane - as well as Pam's dog - had been instrumental in solving that mystery. When they came home from the retreat, they told the story to everyone who would listen. By fall, everybody at the art center had heard it. Their adventure had even earned itself a title. Pam, who was the poet of their painting group, had dubbed it, "A Brush with Murder." She kept urging Jane to write a whodunnit about their experience.

"I'll come first thing in the morning and get the skeleton down, Ruth Alice," Jane said. "I don't know why I didn't listen to Chandler. He's the one with expertise at hanging a show."

"It's okay," Ruth Alice said. "All's well that ends well. I'll see you in the morning. Right now, I'm going to head over to the office. Who knows? Maybe those moments of panic will produce a rush in sales."

"I think that only works with gun sales," Donna said. "Not paintings."

"Thank goodness we don't sell guns at the Art Center!" Pam blurted. Her silk scarf slipped off her shoulder, and she grabbed a corner to toss it back into place. Somehow, she managed to dunk it in her glass of cider. "Hmm, seems I have a wardrobe malfunction," she said. "I'm off to the little ladies room to rinse off this mess. But I'll be glad to relieve you at the punchbowl, Jane, if you feel like you need some downtime after all the excitement."

"I'm okay," Jane said. She checked her phone. "My shift is over in about fifteen minutes, anyway."

Jane waved goodbye to her friends and headed back to the smaller gallery, where she was in charge of the table with the adult refreshments. As soon as she got to the punch bowl, she poured herself a full serving of spiked cider, gulped it down, then refilled the cup. What I really need is some spike without the cider, she thought. But I'm driving myself home, so I better go easy.

Of all the members of their painting group, Jane was considered the most level-headed. A short, trim woman, she'd never married, and she had only herself to arrange all the details of everyday living. Now that she was retired, she arranged her days into an orderly routine of painting, singing in choirs, and embroidery - all activities that she dearly loved. Volunteering at the art center was her way of saying thank you for the wonderful life she lived. As she ladled cider into cups, she felt her back muscles begin to relax. Now that she had something to do with her hands, a job to do, Jane's breathing slowed.

"I saw you talking to that little boy. Is he feeling better?"

Jane looked up at Grace Tanner, an attractive woman with lustrous, platinum hair. She was wearing an airy lilac and pink dress that seemed to float around her body. Standing beside Grace was Betsy Winkle. Both were members of Jane's watercolor painting group, a group of six women that met on Tuesdays in the AAC kitchen. Grace had also been part of their now-famous retreat, "A Brush with Murder."

"That dress looks great on you," Jane said as she refilled Grace's cup. "I don't think I've seen you wear it since the retreat. I thought maybe you'd purged it from your wardrobe because it brought back unpleasant memories."

"You've got a good memory. This is the first time I've worn it since then," Grace said. "But I do like it. And it's not the dress's fault that I let myself get bamboozled by that terrible man."

"Well, I certainly don't think you should let a man get between you and a fabulous dress," Betsy winked, grinning at her mildly ribald remark. "Hey, what was that screaming business about, anyway? The kid just got spooked by the skeleton?"

Jane nodded and sighed. "Yeah, it was really dumb of me to hang that up. I should have known it would scare kids."

Betsy frowned. "Don't beat yourself up," she said. "At Halloween, there are more skeletons scattered around than candy corn. I think that kid was overly sensitive."

Betsy had ear-length brown hair, sensible shoes, and a straightforward, practical view of the world. With a background in occupational therapy, she was generous with her advice and confident about her opinions. Always eager to patch wounds, both medical and emotional, Betsy jumped into every situation with the energy of the Eveready Bunny.

"Dear Jane," Grace said as she reached out to pat Jane's hand. "Anybody who knows you would realize that you never intended to scare anybody. That wouldn't be like you at all."

"You know," Betsy said, as she turned to Grace, "Donna is so right about you."

Grace, clearly puzzled, looked at Betsy. "What do you mean?"

"Whenever Donna tells the story of that retreat, she talks about how you fit your name. Grace. You're so ... well, gracious. All the time. How did your mother know that? To name you that."

Grace sighed. "Oh, will you stop that!"

Jane giggled. "Where are your menfolk, you two? Didn't you tell me you were bringing a date tonight, Grace?"

"We left them over there," Betsy said. She pointed at two men - Betsy's husband Jim and Grace's date, a tall attorney named Edward Walker. The men were talking with Maisie O'Rourke and her husband, Win. Maisie was the sixth member of their watercolor group.

"So, what are you going to do?" Betsy asked. "Take down the skeleton?"

Jane nodded. "Tomorrow morning. I don't want to bring in the ladder tonight."

"That big old ladder behind the stage? I better come and help you," Betsy volunteered. "You shouldn't be lugging around that heavy thing by yourself. And you certainly shouldn't be climbing a ladder without a spotter. That's the classic recipe for broken bones in older people."

"You're right," Jane said. "Ruth Alice offered to help, but I hate to take her away from her desk. She has so much going on, between coordinating this show and getting ready for all the holiday events." Jane looked around the room. "You know, I'm really glad that so many people came out for this reception. But I hate that everybody will remember it as The Night of the Screaming Child."

"Now that'd be a pretty good title for a whodunnit," Betsy said. "Except it needs a real dead body - not just a plastic skeleton - if anybody's going to read it."

Jane groaned. "Please. Do me a favor and don't go there. The last thing we need after all that screaming is a real skeleton in the art closet."

Betsy burst out laughing, spraying out cider in the process. Jane handed her a napkin. As she mopped her chin, Betsy said, "There, that's your title. Skeleton in the Art Closet."

CHAPTER TWO

The Atkinsville Art Center opened at 10 a.m. on Saturdays. At quarter 'til, Jane sat on the metal bench outside the Gallery Building's front entrance, gazing at the dandelions going to seed around the edges of the bushes. Jane decided the weeds were symbolic: Under the former director, the center had started to go to seed. Thank goodness Ruth Alice was running the center now. Under her skilled and generous leadership, the arts were beginning to flourish again. It was time to weed this area, Jane thought.

The Gallery Building had originally been a school, a red brick building that housed elementary through high school students. As the town's population grew, a second building was added, which was now called the Studio Annex. Together with a freestanding gymnasium, where longtime residents remembered playing basketball and dancing at proms, the three buildings had been the rural town's entire school system. Eventually they were replaced by schools located closer to burgeoning subdivisions. These old buildings had stood, unused and neglected, until a group of artists and art-lovers bought them for a ceremonial dollar. Volunteers had transformed the complex, using donated supplies and sweat equity, into a modern gallery space, classrooms, and an event venue.

As she waited, Jane relived last night's reception in her head. Thankfully, she hadn't gone to bed dwelling on the scene. She'd been able to shut off her brain - probably thanks to the spike in the cider - and get a decent night's sleep. But now, as she stared at the weeds dotting the cement walkway, she felt totally responsible and very guilty about hanging the stupid skeleton. What was I thinking? Maybe I should come in Monday and do some weeding. She was feeling like she ought to pay penance for messing up the opening of the show.

Betsy parked her car and joined Jane on the bench. When Ruth Alice arrived promptly at 10, Jane stood up. "Betsy volunteered to come and help me get the skeleton down," Jane told her. "So you won't have to eat up your morning."

Ruth Alice let them all into the building and turned on the lights. "Oh, you know I don't mind helping," she said. "I'm always glad to support our volunteers. But if you ladies can handle it by yourselves, I'll get busy making out the bank deposit. We really did have a sales rush last night. We sold 29 pieces, and two people said they were going to come by this morning to purchase. It's probably the best opening night we've ever had."

"Way to go!" Betsy said and slapped the flat of her hand against Ruth Alice's palm. "See, Jane, that skeleton was worth its weight in gold. Maybe you should leave it up? That little boy probably won't be back."

"No, but his mother has a piece in the show," Jane said. "So, she'll probably be back, and we told her we were taking it down."

"Besides," Ruth Alice said, "school groups are coming to see the show. Other kids might get spooked, too." Ruth Alice glanced at the clock mounted above the doorway of her office. "Speaking of kids - two Girl Scout troops are coming this morning. So, I better get moving." Ruth Alice scurried off toward her desk, which was piled with papers and brochures.

Jane and Betsy found the ladder propped against the back wall of the dusty storage area behind the stage. The ladder was as heavy as it was awkward, and Jane was grateful that Betsy had volunteered to help. Of all the painters in their watercolor group, Betsy was probably the strongest. Jane always pictured her marching through life with the hardy, no-nonsense attitude of a character in a PBS show about the Scottish Highlands.

They managed to get the ladder down the creaky steps and into the back door of the Central Gallery. After they'd set it up beside the skeleton, Jane climbed up, while Betsy held onto the legs. The ladder swayed and groaned with Jane's every step.

"I wonder how old this ladder is," Betsy said. "The wood looks really old. I bet it's been here as long as the building. This place was built when? In the 1930s? How long does wood last, anyway?"

"Let's talk about that later, shall we?" Jane said. She reached up to pull the skeleton's neck out of the rope that held it. Then, holding the skull, she lowered it into Betsy's arms. Betsy gathered up the wired-together bones and lowered the skeleton to the floor.

Jane reached up again to flip the rope off the hook attached to the ceiling. "I don't think I can reach the hook to unscrew it," she said. "Chandler screwed it in for me, and he's taller than either of us. You think it would be okay to leave it there?"

"Sure, if anybody notices it, they'll think it's left over from a hanging plant."

"Hmm," Jane said. "Not a bad idea. Maybe we should go get a plant and hang it up?"

"With a Halloween theme?" Barb said. "Maybe poison ivy?"

Jane giggled. "Don't make me laugh when I'm up here," she said. "Every time this ladder creaks, I'm thinking, 'It's probably not going to break today. But it's probably been here for nearly a century. So then again, it might.'"

After folding the ladder and storing it behind the stage, Jane and Betsy went back to the Central Gallery to retrieve the skeleton and the rope.

"Where should we put this stuff?" Betsy held up the rope.

"Here, I'll take that," Jane said. "There's a box of rope in that closet behind the door to the tunnel - where all the tools are."

When Jane came back into the gallery, she found Betsy waltzing around the room, holding the skeleton like her dance partner. "We did the mash," she sang as she twirled, "the monster mash." Betsy grinned. "Alas, there's only one of you, Yorick. So poor Janie will have to dance by herself."

The sound of the front door opening interrupted Betsy's song and dance. Jane peeked into the hall and announced, "The Girl Scouts are here.

Let's go through the tunnel so the kids don't see the skeleton. I want to put Yorick back where I found him."

Jane and Betsy carried the skeleton down the narrow steps to a damp storage room that smelled like clay and mold. From there, they entered the earthen tunnel that connected each of the buildings in the old school complex. At the door that led up to the Studio Annex, Betsy grabbed the doorknob. "It's locked," she said to Jane.

"I know the combination," Jane said. "Chandler told me. So I could get in when we were getting supplies to set up the show."

"You've been in this tunnel by yourself?" Betsy said. She wrinkled up her nose.

"It's the quickest way to get to the Studio Annex," Jane said.

"But it's kinda creepy. Don't you think? Especially when you pass that locked room off to the side."

"You mean the old bomb shelter? Yeah, I guess it is kinda creepy. It smells down here, and there are always noises - probably from critters that live in the walls." Jane shrugged. "But I live alone. If I let myself get creeped out by stuff like that, I'd be hiding under my covers every night."

Betsy held Yorick so Jane could punch in the combination to the lock. They went up the wooden steps and entered the spacious atrium of the Studio Annex. Jane noticed that the door to the drawing classroom was ajar. That's odd, she thought. She was sure she'd closed the door on Friday morning, after she'd gotten the skeleton. There weren't any classes scheduled in that room after lunch on Friday afternoons. Maybe one of the instructors had come in to get something?

"Remind me to tell Ruth Alice that somebody keeps leaving that door open," Jane said. "It's a waste of money and electricity." In this building, the studios and classrooms were heated and air conditioned, but the big atrium wasn't.

There was no need to turn on the light in the drawing classroom because morning sun from ceiling-high windows bathed the room. All the easels were folded and stored against the side wall, just as they'd been when

Jane had come in to get the skeleton. To the right of the easels, the back wall was covered by a wide chalk board. It was clean - erased and washed - just like it was when Jane had last seen it. Along the wall to their right was a narrow walk-in closet where art supplies were stored.

"It's blacker than sin in here," Betsy said as Jane opened the closet door. "Is there a light somewhere?"

"Yeah, wait a minute while I feel for it," Jane said. She stuck her hand into a recess in the shelf on the right and fumbled around until she finally managed to locate the light switch. "Whoever designed this art supply closet didn't make it easy to turn on the light."

"Shall I tuck Yorick in beside his friend?" Betsy asked.

"Huh?"

"Over there. On the shelf," Betsy said. "Where the other skeleton is."

Jane blinked. Sure enough, there was another skeleton lying across the shelf at the back of the closet. The thing was on its back, lying on a woolen blanket. Its skull was looking up, and its arms were crossed across its chest, in the classic skeletal pose.

Jane swallowed. "Um. There wasn't another skeleton when I was here on Friday," Jane looked at Betsy. "And I'm sure I locked this building behind me."

Betsy shrugged. "Well, someone must have brought it in, later," she said. "Maybe they let the students take home the skeletons? You know, like a classroom lending library? Kinda gruesome. But the students need models to draw from. And modeling rates for a skeleton are probably dirt cheap. Get it? Dirt. As in, buried six feet under."

Jane's frown did not loosen. "A lending library for bones? I've never taken a drawing class here, but I kind of doubt it." She pushed the blanket to slide the new skeleton farther back on the shelf so there'd be room for Yorick. But the bones weren't wired together. They jiggled and fell apart. "You know, this skeleton doesn't feel like it's made of the same material," Jane said. "And the bones aren't wired together. They're just lying here on the blanket."

Betsy draped Yorick over her shoulder so she could pick up one of the loose bones. Some flecks of dirt fell off the bone. "This isn't the same material," she said.

Even in the dim light of the ceiling fixture, Jane could see that Betsy's face had gone ashen.

"I'm pretty sure these bones are made of bone," Betsy said. "As in: The kind you get from a dead body!"

CHAPTER THREE

On Saturday night, sleep did not come restfully to Jane. She woke at midnight all sweaty, with the vague notion that she'd had a disturbing dream. She tossed and turned until she finally managed to doze off again. At 2:30, she awoke again. But this time, she was freezing. Evidently, she'd thrown off the covers. She got up and padded to the bathroom. Of course, her exit disturbed Lotus, the female Siamese cat who usually slept calmly at the foot of her bed.

If Jane was getting up, Lotus assumed it must be morning. And morning meant wet cat food. Trilling, Lotus jumped off the bed and followed Jane to the bathroom. When Jane headed toward her bedroom, rather than the kitchen, Lotus began complaining. Piteously. The noise woke Levi, Jane's male Siamese, who usually spent the night downstairs on the living room couch. He jogged up the carpeted stairs and started a duet with Lotus.

Ignoring both of them, Jane slid under her covers. Outraged, both cats kept up their vocal protests until she got up, shooed both of them out of her bedroom, and shut the door. That magnified their outrage. Jane covered her ears. Why is it, she thought, that I have to strain to hear my friends' voices without my hearing aids, but I can hear these cats with crystal clarity?

After what seemed like hours, either the cats hushed or Jane managed to fall asleep in spite of the din. But the sleep that came was more disturbing than it was deep. Jane was in a dark closet that smelled like paint and linseed oil. The shelves were cluttered with menacing art supplies: large, terrifying scissors, glinting X-acto blades, and pencils with dagger-sharp points. A skeleton dangled from the ceiling by a noose. It danced as it dangled. The skull grinned, the jaw clacked up and down to the tune of "The Monster Mash." Long bumpy finger bones motioned to Jane, inviting her to climb up a rickety ladder and jump into the skeleton's wired-together arm bones. When Jane refused the gruesome invitation, the skeleton began to howl. It hopped to the ground, flipped its noose off the hook on the ceiling, and swung it above its skull. As the noose whirled, it became a lasso. The lasso threatened to envelop Jane, and she fled from the closet and slammed the door shut. But it opened with a creaking sound, despite her repeated attempts to fasten it. Jane shut the door again. And again. On the other side of the door, the skeleton wailed.

Jane sat up in bed. She needed to go to the bathroom again. She shouldn't have drunk that cup of tea before bed. But chamomile was soothing, and her nerves had been jangled. Knowing the cats would start up again if she opened her door, she decided to hold it in and try to resume her sleep.

She couldn't. Her brain was wide awake. Jane played back the day from the time she arrived at AAC until she'd finally left at around 4 in the afternoon.

Thankfully, the town police had agreed to wait until the bus was repacked with Girl Scouts before surrounding the AAC complex with yellow crime tape. Jane and Betsy had been asked to stay, of course, so they could be interviewed about the discovery of the skeleton. Betsy had been right. The bones really were from a human body. At about 2 p.m., a forensics expert from the university had arrived to inspect them. The scientist said she'd have to do some measurements, but she was pretty sure the skeleton belonged to a child, maybe around the age of 10. That rattled everybody. A genuine skeleton from a genuine dead body was bad enough. But a child? The forensics expert also said the bones were old; she couldn't be sure how old until she ran some tests. Maybe 40 or 50 years old, maybe older.

There had been some speculation that the child might have been buried when the art center was still a school complex. That would date them from before AAC had acquired the buildings and begun renovating them. When was that? The 1970s? 1980s? But still, Jane thought, that doesn't make any sense. Children don't get buried at a school. And how did a child's skeleton end up in the art closet? For that matter, when did it end up there? It hadn't been there on Friday when Jane had gotten the plastic replica. Jane was sure of that. The police had asked her repeatedly about whether she might have missed seeing it when she'd taken the plastic skeleton out of the closet. What were the chances? How could anyone miss seeing an entire skeleton?

When light finally peeked through the curtains, Jane got up and showered. Her watercolor group was meeting at Pam's for brunch and a paint-out. Everybody was bringing a dish. Although they were in the deep South, it was early November and much too chilly to swim in Pam's outdoor pool. But the greenery around the pool was lush and attractive. Pam had plenty of wrought iron benches and pool chairs. The painters were planning to set up their easels and paint outside, en plein air.

Jane had volunteered to bring homemade "angel" biscuits for the potluck. She was going to use a recipe that she'd gotten from a talented cook when she attended the now-infamous watercolor retreat in South Carolina. The biscuits were easy to make and reliably light and flaky. They required about 30 minutes to bake, and they tasted best when they were fresh, so Jane needed to get them into the oven by 10 or 10:30 to arrive in time for brunch. After she'd dressed in some comfortable pants and a long-sleeved tee, Jane went downstairs. In spite of their irritation with Jane, Lotus and Levi consented to eat the wet cat food that she scooped into bowls for them. She fixed a cup of black coffee and toasted half a bagel to tide herself over, then sat at the kitchen counter to eat.

She couldn't get her mind off the discovery of the child's bones. Maybe there was an old cemetery that abutted AAC? But if the child was buried in a cemetery, how did its bones get into the art closet in the Studio Annex? It didn't make a bit of sense.

Jane retrieved the Sunday newspaper from the orange plastic box attached to her mailbox. She skimmed the contents, then spread out the

New York Times crossword. But she couldn't concentrate on the crossword clues. She kept puzzling over the clues involving the skeleton. When she glanced at her phone, she realized that it was past time to start the biscuits.

Recognizing that she was distracted, Jane made herself check the recipe three times to be sure she'd measured out correct amounts. As soon as the biscuits were baked, Jane transferred them to a basket, wrapped a clean dish towel around them to keep them hot, and put them into the car. She drove halfway to Pam's house before she realized that she hadn't put her easel or art supplies in the trunk, so she had to turn around and drive home to get them.

As soon as she opened the gate to Pam's yard, Jane was assaulted by Tillie. The big black dog jumped up, balanced her gargantuan paws against Jane's chest, and licked Jane's chin. Holding the basket of biscuits above her head, Jane edged inside the gate and planted her backside against the deck's railing, so Tillie couldn't knock her down.

"Here's Shirley Holmes," Pam announced as she hurried up the deck stairs to rescue Jane. "Get down, you big lummox," she said to Tillie, who - as usual - ignored her. Pam took the basket of biscuits and started down to the pool area with it.

Grace had followed Pam to Jane's rescue. She shooed Tillie aside and shut the gate behind Jane. Tillie showed her appreciation by leaping on Grace. The dog deposited an impressive glob of drool on Grace's nose.

"Ugh," Grace said, as she wiped off the glob. She glanced behind her to be sure Pam couldn't hear. "I just don't know how she puts up with this every day." As if to demonstrate the problem, Tillie jumped up again and swabbed Grace's ear with her tongue.

Jane giggled. "I don't know. Pam lives alone in this big house. Tillie must be good company." She shrugged. "Wouldn't be my cup of chamomile. I've never been a dog person, myself."

"Hear you found another skeleton," Donna called as Jane came down the deck stairs with Tillie bumping against her calves. Donna was sitting in a metal lawn chair by the side of the pool. "And this time, it was the real McCoy. Or I guess I should say, the dead McCoy."

"I gather you've already told everybody about the skeleton in the art closet?" Jane said to Betsy, who was sitting beside Donna. Maisie was sitting on Betsy's other side. All three of them held the remnants of a mimosa in plastic stemmed glasses.

"I was planning to wait for you to get here before I told the story," Betsy said. "But it took you forever." She looked at Jane and shrugged. "We were sitting here, talking, and the skeleton - er, the story of the skeleton - just slipped out."

"Actually, it was the first thing you said when you opened the gate," Maisie said. "Before hello." A wide smile spread across Maisie's face, erasing all of her features. Jane, as always, marveled at Maisie's resemblance to the Cheshire Cat - just a topknot of grey-brown hair above a gigantic smile.

Maisie started laughing. Whenever she laughed, and especially when she'd had a bit to drink, she snorted. And the more she snorted, the more she laughed. Pam started to giggle, and the mirth became contagious. Donna gave her gruff little "heh, heh" laugh. Maisie snorted again. Grace, ever sensitive to other people's feelings, covered her mouth with her hand. Jane couldn't help but notice that Grace was smiling under her fingers.

"Exactly how many mimosas have y'all had?" Jane asked.

"This may have been our shecond pitcher," Pam slurred. "Or third-ish. Who's counting? I bought a gallon of orange juice for the bunch. I mean, brunch." She emptied the rest of the pitcher into a glass and handed it to Jane. "Here. Let's toast to Yorick's little brother."

"We were starving," Betsy said. "The mimosas helped us stave off our hunger pangs. And, you know what they say: five servings of fruits and veggies a day. It's important for mature women to eat - and drink - healthy."

Donna got up, reached for the basket of biscuits on the picnic table, and peeled off the dish towel. She looked at Jane. "So, did your mother like to solve murder mysteries, too?"

"What do you mean?" Jane asked. She took a long sip of her mimosa to catch up with the rest of the group - no fun to be the only sober painter in this group.

"I remember you saying that you got your love of baking from her," Donna said as she helped herself to a biscuit and passed the basket to Maisie.

"I thought maybe you inherited your talent for solving murder mysteries from her, too."

Jane was about to point out that murder mysteries were not part of her matrilineal line. She'd only ever solved one, that being the one at their art retreat in spring. She opened her mouth, but thought better of it and took another sip of her mimosa. Fine details were going to be lost on this group.

After brunch and another pitcher of mimosas, they set up their easels around the pool. Jane pulled out her large brush. Given the mimosas, she figured it was a good day to paint loose and wet.

"You know," Betsy said, "I was thinking about that AAC project with the school kids. The one where our art docents helped the kids study a local landmark and bring it to life. You helped with that project, didn't you, Pam?"

"Yup," Pam said. "The kids researched the history of the old school buildings at AAC. Then they painted pictures of them or made scale models. And wrote a play."

"Didn't you tell me that you found out some odd things about the Studio Annex?" Betsy asked. "Like, the town women would come and can their green beans? And the town doctor would do medical appointments there?"

Pam chuckled. "Yes, the ladies of Atkinsville would bring their jars of jelly and vegetables to the big atrium in the Studio Annex. They'd have a sort of community canning bee."

Betsy cocked her head. "But what was it you told me about the town doctor? He used to set up shop in there?"

"He did," Pam said. "Believe it or not. He did a sort of tonsillectomy assembly line. The kids would file in, and the doc would cut out their tonsils."

"You're making that up!" Grace said. "What parent would let their kid get their tonsils out at school, like that?"

Pam shrugged. "Well, it was a simpler time. This was a small town. A very small town. Everybody knew each other. The kids needed to get their tonsils out to avoid getting bad colds or infections. And the easiest place to assemble a bunch of kids was at school."

"It doesn't sound sanitary, does it?" Grace said.

"I guess they could sanitize the atrium, same as a doctor's office," Pam said. "Anyway, I'm not making this up. We found a newspaper article in the Heritage Room at the library. It announced the annual Tonsil Day at school. Even had a photo of two nurses who were taking kids' temperatures at the event."

"What do you think they did with all the tonsils?" Maisie asked. She chuckled.

"In the photo, there was a big bucket on the floor," Pam said. "I bet the doctor dumped the tonsils into the bucket. Then somebody took it out back and emptied it."

Maisie laughed out loud. "Maybe that's why the grass always looks so lush behind the art center!" She began to snort. Of course, this set Donna off, which made Jane, Betsy, and Pam giggle.

"Oh, gross!" Grace said.

"You know," Betsy said. "Maybe that's how the child's skeleton got there."

"What? You think the doc's blade slipped? And he buried the kid at school?" Pam said.

"That makes no sense," Grace said. "Surely the parents would have noticed if their child didn't come home from school."

Betsy cocked her head. "You never know. In those days, it was all farming out here. Big farm families. Kids walked miles and miles to school. They probably stopped to play in creeks on hot days. Or wandered into the woods. If a kid didn't come home from school one day, maybe it wasn't so unusual? They wouldn't have had the crime-detection techniques we have today. So, it would've been pretty easy to cover up a botched medical procedure by making a victim disappear."

"That's so sad," Grace said. "I know we're all making jokes about the skeleton. But I feel sorry for the child, don't you?"

"It is sad," Betsy agreed. "Not to mention criminal. But we don't know who the child was. Or how he got there. Or even whether he was a he. All we know is those were real bones from a real child. Without knowing anything else, it's hard for me to get emotionally invested in the kid."

"Especially after a few mimosas," Jane remarked.

"It sounds to me like one of those TV detective series," Donna said. "The Case of the Deadly Tonsils."

CHAPTER FOUR

On Tuesdays, the watercolor group usually gathered in AAC's kitchen to paint. Jane wondered if they'd be allowed into the building today, since the police had surrounded all three buildings with yellow crime tape on Saturday.

She called the art center, and Ruth Alice answered. "How's everything going?" After exchanging pleasantries, Jane asked, "Is AAC open today?"

"Two of the buildings - the Gallery Building and Studio Annex - are still blocked off," Ruth Alice said. "The police let me come in to work in my office. But nobody else is allowed in. I hate it. Nobody can get in to see the show."

Jane reminded Ruth Alice that the watercolor painters were scheduled to meet in the kitchen.

"I forgot all about your group meeting on Tuesdays," Ruth Alice said. "I guess I'm still flustered by all this police stuff. But you can't get into this building today, and we don't have another space for you to work. The Old Gym is open, but the Art Angelas are working in the basketball court. I guess you could set up in the hallway, but it's not very big. And the Angelas are using all the tables."

The Art Angelas were the auxiliary group that raised money for the art center. They were getting ready for their annual Santa Sale, their biggest fundraiser. Every year, in mid-November, the Angelas transformed the former basketball court in the Old Gym into a store to sell their hand-crafted holiday decorations. It was a popular event and attracted shoppers from as far away as Atlanta. Since the sale received so much foot traffic, the watercolor painters had begun using the hallway to set up a painting exhibit during the Santa Store. That way, shoppers had to walk through their exhibit to get to the store. The intersection of the two events had definitely increased sales of their paintings, and AAC benefited by getting a 30 percent commission on each sale.

"I'm sorry," Ruth Alice said. "I should have called you."

"That's okay," Jane said. "I know how you feel. I'm still flustered, too. I'll let the other painters know. Maybe we'll use the time to go check out the hallway. See if it's ready for us to set up our exhibit."

After she hung up, Jane texted the members of her watercolor group: Kitchen closed today. Let's meet at 10 in Old Gym n plan exhibit.

Jane put on a jacket but took it off as soon as she left the house. It was a pretty day, mild and crisp with a blue sky and a slight breeze - the kind of day that made her glad she lived in the South. When Jane pulled into the AAC parking lot, the door to the Old Gym was open. She didn't spot any of the cars that belonged to the watercolor painters, so she figured she was the first to arrive. Gathering up her notebook and pen, she tucked her car keys into her pocket and went into the building. She figured she'd check out the hallway and maybe say hello to the Angelas while she waited for the watercolor group to arrive.

In the hallway, she flipped on the lights, set her notebook and pen on a table by the door, and started poking around. The hallway definitely needed cleaning. Leaves and debris had blown in, and the windowsills were covered in dust and cobwebs. A broken chair had been dumped in the corner behind the door, and there were a couple of empty cartons piled against the wall. One of the bulbs in the ceiling fixture had burnt out, so the hallway was dim. It was a good thing the painters were going to meet here this morning, Jane thought. They needed to get this space tidy before bringing over their paintings.

Unlike the disordered hallway, the basketball court felt inviting. The large room had high ceilings with wooden cross beams that dropped down and formed triangular shapes. An ancient basketball hoop - a touch of nostalgia - hung over the back wall. Bordered on the sides by painted wooden bleachers, the whole area had an old-fashioned, homey feel. Thanks to all the holiday trimmings, it smelled like Christmas - a combination of pine and cinnamon.

The room was buzzing with activity. A dozen or so tables were spread out, and 10 or 15 women were at work on their holiday crafts. Jane looked around and waved to some familiar faces. A tall silver-haired woman sat at a sewing machine, which hummed under her skilled hands. Beside her lay a pile of quilted squares. Jane guessed they were destined to be placemats. At a table, a woman was painting a sign. Stacked on the floor beside her were pieces of scrap wood. A few completed signs were drying, and Jane smiled at a snowman holding the words, 'I'm dreaming of a white Christmas.' Along one side of the room, three tables stood end-to-end. They held boxes of feathers, coils of wire, and jars of sequins. Jane guessed this was an assembly line for making bird ornaments.

The table closest to Jane was the wreath-making station. It was piled with greenery, circular forms, red and green bows, silver bells, sticks of vanilla, and pine cones. Two women sat across from each other on either side of the table. Recognizing them, Jane walked over and said hello.

Cathy Barron grinned. "What's this I hear? You discovered another dead body?" Cathy was a retired schoolteacher who had taught at the same elementary school as Grace. "In the art closet, of all places!" Cathy continued. "Who would have thought such a thing? You've become quite the sleuth."

Jane knew that Cathy played in a bridge group for retired teachers, and so did Grace. "Let me guess," Jane said. "You played bridge with Grace yesterday."

Cathy chuckled. "No, Donna spilled the beans." She nodded at a table in the far corner, where Donna was seated. Jane hadn't noticed her when she came in. "She's working on her Nessies." Every year, Donna made ornaments in the shape of Norwegian trolls, with oversized noses and pointy felted hats. They were big sellers.

"I'm glad it wasn't me that found the body," said Roberta Roberts, the woman sitting across from Cathy. Roberta was Cathy's sister-in-law. She was also a retired teacher. "The thought gives me the willies. That's why I refuse to go through that tunnel. Who knows what you're going to find under these buildings, as old as this place is? I told Robert that even if it's pouring down rain, I'd rather get soaking wet than go down there."

Robert was Roberta's husband. Robert and Roberta Roberts. As if their names weren't confusing enough, the couple had given all four of their children names that began with R - Robbie Jr., Robin, Rhonda, and Rosalie. Since Jane's last name, Roland, began with an R, she always gave an inward sigh of relief when she bumped into Roberta. Thank goodness her parents hadn't adopted a similar system for names!

Both Roberta and Cathy were what you'd call pleasingly plump. They had curly brown-and-grey hair and tortoise-shell reading glasses. Both were wearing white tee shirts and red aprons. Although they were related by marriage, not by biology, Jane thought they looked like sisters - like twin versions of Mrs. Santa. Actually, Jane reflected, most of AAC's members were older, retired residents of the town, and nearly all the active volunteers, like the Angelas, were older women. The Angelas only had one man in their group. That was Chandler, AAC's show curator, and he loved to brag about being the token Angela. Although there was no rule about whether men could join the auxiliary, Jane wondered if the group's name kept most men away. Chandler wasn't the least bit deterred, though. He loved to introduce himself as Mr. Angela.

Jane walked over to Donna's table. "Did you get my text?"

"What text?" Donna asked. She chuckled. "I guess not."

"We're meeting in the hallway today," Jane cocked her head in the direction of the hallway. "The Gallery Building is still off limits. Did you see the crime tape around it?"

"I wondered if they were going to let us in," Donna said. "I was just about to walk up there and see."

"Ruth Alice said no," Jane said. "And it's probably just as well. The hallway is a mess. It definitely needs some attention before we hang our exhibit."

Donna finished gluing a pom-pom nose on a Nessie with a glittering conical hat. She showed him to Jane. "Cute, huh?"

Jane smiled. "He's definitely got personality. Do you name your Nessies?"

"Everybody asks me that. This one is called Loch." Donna gave her gruff little laugh. "Actually, they're all called Loch. It's a good line. A smiling customer is a buying customer."

"There you are!" Pam called as she bustled over to join them. "I saw your notebook in the hall," she said to Jane. "I figured you were in here."

"Anybody else here yet?" Jane said.

"Yes, everybody's here," Pam said. "Betsy's gone to get a broom."

"Good," Jane said. "That hallway could use sweeping."

Donna untied her apron and laid it on the Nessie table. She picked up her pocketbook, and the three of them began walking toward the hallway.

"You know how we were talking about the tonsillectomies they used to do in the Studio Annex?" Pam said as they walked. "And how they might have something to do with the skeleton of that child?"

Donna chuckled. "Yup. The Case of the Deadly Tonsils."

"I was thinking about the tonsillectomy theory," Pam said. "You know, that doctor's family still lives here. Out in the county, on that land that used to be a peach orchard. As a matter of fact, his grandson is a doctor."

"Let me guess," Donna said, "a bone doctor?"

Pam rolled her eyes. "Yes! How'd you guess? He's an orthopedic surgeon."

"Do you know him?" Jane asked.

"I've met him," Pam said. "He and his wife came to the school and talked with the kids when we were researching the history of the Studio Annex building. They have a collection of old surgical instruments that they brought to show the kids. Nice people. They're both members of AAC."

"I think I know them," Donna said. "Didn't they help at the Summerfest reception?"

Jane's brain began to churn. "I wonder if he'd let us talk to him? I mean, we have no reason to believe the child's bones had anything to do with a botched tonsillectomy. It's just a wild possibility. So, we aren't threatening to besmirch the doctor's family name."

26

"Yet," Donna said.

"What do you mean?" Jane asked.

"You aren't going to besmirch the family name. Yet. But if you find out something, you will," Donna said.

"We'll probably see him at the opening of our exhibit," Pam said. "He and his wife come to it every year. I'll introduce you, and we can ask him if he'll talk to us about his grandfather and Tonsil Day. But if we discover anything shady and let the police know, then Donna's right. The whole town will know this guy's got a skeleton in his family closet."

Jane shrugged. "That's true. Although - to be literal - it's not in his family closet. It's in the art closet."

CHAPTER FIVE

The opening reception for both the Santa Store and the watercolor exhibit was held on the third Friday night in November, the week before Thanksgiving, from 7 to 9. The Angelas had baked typical holiday goodies, like gingerbread men and frosted sugar cookies in the shape of wreaths and ornaments. They'd also made Southern specialties - fluffy divinity, mini pecan pies, and red velvet cake. The watercolor painters contributed savories with a Southern flair - cheddar crackers, fried chicken tenders, and finger sandwiches stuffed with pimento cheese. Jane had made smaller versions of her angel biscuits and stuffed them with slices of ham.

Four large rectangular tables, covered with crisp white tablecloths, were set up inside the basketball court along the wall that separated the court from the hallway. As Jane added her plate of ham biscuits to the savory table, she helped herself to a cheddar cracker and admired the gleaming buffet. The food was arranged on silver and crystal platters, and it looked sumptuous - a feast for the eye. Each table was bedecked with stiff green holly leaves, red berries, and pine cones coated with glitter. As beautiful as the buffet looked, the aroma was the main attraction: Fried chicken! Tangy cheeses! Yeast! Vanilla! Sugar!

As guests entered the building, Chandler - dressed in a Santa costume - greeted them in the hallway with a theatrical "ho, ho, ho." Since Chandler was a slim fellow with a clean-shaven chin, he was definitely not the embodiment of the classical Santa. To compensate, he'd padded his waist with a pillow to give himself a corpulent torso and donned a fake white beard. He stood by the door beside a round table covered with a red and green cloth. On the table was a large thermos of hot chocolate, a plate of mini-marshmallows, and a galvanized basin filled with bottles of wine and crushed ice.

Following his "ho, ho, ho," Chandler offered drinks to each of the entering visitors: "Would you prefer 'white as my beard'? Or 'red as Rudolph's nose'?" If a guest was clearly underage or declined the wine, Chandler offered hot chocolate. Some of the children refused all of the drinks, but gleefully picked up a handful of marshmallows, which Chandler described as "puffy snow from the rooftops."

After the beverages, visitors were invited to tour the painting exhibit with one of the watercolor painters. Jane usually started her tours by talking about the group's themed display. Every year, the painters agreed on a subject, and they each did one painting for their group display. This year, they'd set up a still life with apples, pumpkins, and grapes in a cornucopia basket. Visitors usually remarked at how differently each painter's handling of the same subject was. Jane had begun with a barely-visible underpainting. Then she'd slowly built up layer after layer of color until a vivid, realistic painting emerged. Pam had started by splattering the paper with flecks of gold and maroon, rather like the splashes of pool water that her dog shook onto unwary visitors. Her finished painting seemed to be spangled with glints of color and light. Maisie had blurred the edges of the objects so they seemed to bleed together. Jane thought the finished effect resembled fruit salad rather than a still life, but she kept her assessment to herself when she led visitors through the display.

In the basketball court, the Angelas had set up a cash register and wrapping station at one corner of their Santa Store, and they staffed it with their volunteers. That meant Ruth Alice was free to mingle with the gathering crowd. Jane peeked through the hallway door and waved at the director. Unlike the previous director, Ruth Alice understood how important it was to forge relationships with AAC's supporters. She greeted all the volunteers and artists by name. Jane marveled: How does she keep them all in her memory? A thriving art center requires dozens of volunteers and at least as many artists. In addition to painters, AAC had a popular pottery studio, a jewelry-makers guild, woodworkers, and sculptors, as well as writers, textile artists, and book-makers. It astonished Jane that Ruth Alice could remember all these people and greet them by name, especially since she'd only been the director for a few months.

By 8:30, the Old Gym was swirling with visitors. Jane had no idea how many people were in the building. Although the Angelas kept refilling the food, they were running low on some of the baked items, so they'd begun to combine the various desserts to keep the platters from looking scanty. Jane noted that there were more empty wine bottles tucked under Chandler's table than full bottles in the basin.

Jane was showing a young woman one of the paintings that she'd done. It was her most unusual work, a portrait of her cat Levi peeking out of a brown paper bag. The bag was one side of a crinkled grocery sack which Jane had glued onto the paper. Although she often painted her cats, Jane had never incorporated collage into one of her paintings.

"I must have repainted that darn bag three times, but I couldn't get it right," Jane explained to the young woman, who had introduced herself as Susan McDaniel. "I scrubbed at the paper so much that I was afraid I'd make holes in it."

"I've heard that it's impossible to fix a mistake in a watercolor," Susan said.

"Not impossible," Jane said. "But difficult. There's a saying that watercolor is like life - you can't go back. That saying's not completely true," Jane added. "In watercolor, you can lift off the pigment with a wet brush or a Mr. Clean sponge. You have to be gentle, though, or you'll destroy the paper. Or make the colors run together so they look like muddy porridge."

Susan nodded and sipped her wine.

"I was about to give up and throw this painting out," Jane continued, "but I really liked the way the cat's face came out. Then Maisie - she's another painter in our group - suggested this collage idea. I figured I had nothing to lose, so I tried it."

"Wouldn't it be nice if you could glue on a solution when you got frustrated with life?" Susan chuckled. "It's wonderful that you work with a group of painters who can help you solve problems. That's the advantage of working in a group," she said. "I work in a chem lab at the university, and I'm always amazed at how another grad student will come up with a solution to a problem that has stymied me for days."

Jane grinned. "I suppose that chem labs are all about 'solutions'!"

"Hah - good pun!" Susan said. "You know, I really do like the way this painting turned out. It's so 'cat,' if you know what I mean. My cat has a mischievous expression, just like this one. It reminds me of the way she crawls into every...."

Susan stopped mid-word as a wine bottle zinged across the hallway and crashed into one of Donna's paintings. The glass protecting the painting shattered and fell tinkling to the floor. Everyone in the hallway froze. Jane searched for the origin of the missile and saw a big, bulky man standing in front of Chandler's table. The man's face was red, and he was shouting and waving his arms wildly.

Most of the visitors turned toward the commotion. But Donna and Grace rushed over to the painting. Donna pulled it off its hook to examine the damage, and Grace dabbed off the wine with a napkin. Betsy came charging over with a wastebasket and started gathering up broken bits of glass.

"Excuse me," Jane said to the young woman, "I think I'd better get the director."

Ducking into the basketball court, Jane scanned the crowd. The noise of the crash evidently hadn't penetrated the din of voices in this room, since nobody was gaping at the door to the hallway. Jane spotted Ruth Alice in a cluster of people and caught her eye and beckoned. Ruth Alice cocked her head as if to ask if the summons was urgent. Jane grimaced and formed the silent word, "now," with her lips. Ruth Alice excused herself and hurried toward Jane.

"Chandler's got a situation," Jane said. "You better come."

When they reached Chandler's table, the bulky man was still shouting. He looked like an older man, Jane thought - maybe in his 60's. He had a stocky build, a bulging nose, and a comb-over of grey hair. He wasn't dressed in evening clothes like most of the visitors. Instead, he was wearing a brown suede jacket over a button-down shirt. A tiny, white-haired woman stood beside him. She was also wearing an outdoor jacket and a woolen scarf.

"Tony, you heard this fellow," the tiny woman was saying. Her voice was controlled, as if she was trying to calm the bulky man. "He doesn't know anything about it."

This woman's voice may be quiet and even, Jane thought, but the venom in her eyes is terrifying. It reminded her of the saying: 'If looks could kill....'

"That's what they all say," the man huffed. "I'm getting sick of this run-around. Where's the guy in charge? That Parsnip guy?"

"I'm the Director of the Atkinsville Art Center." Ruth Alice stepped forward. "How can I help you?"

"I just came from that other building, that gallery place or whatever it's called," the man said as he waved in the general direction of the Gallery Building. "And they told me to come down here. But I don't see that guy. And I'm sure you're going to tell me the same thing." His voice turned into a sing-song, in mocking imitation of a woman's voice: "There's nothing I can do. I'm only a volunteer."

The man stamped his foot as he roared. "Well, I want to speak to the head of this place. Now!" He punctuated his demand by jabbing a thick finger in the direction of Ruth Alice's nose.

"I am the head of this place. Now." Ruth Alice said, her voice calm and firm.

The tiny woman jumped in: "Tony's painting was stolen. It wasn't hanging on any of the walls up there. Somebody took us to look for it behind the stage, but it wasn't there, either. I'm Tony's wife. I want you to know this has gone on for months. Tony's called and left message after message. That other man gave us his cell phone, but he never answers and he never returns Tony's call." She pursed her lips together and fairly hissed, "Extremely rude, if you ask me."

"You're saying that you had a painting in the show, but you didn't see it in either gallery?" Ruth Alice asked.

Jane said, "Maybe I can help. Chandler and I hung the show. I'm sure none of the artwork was missing. We both checked the list of entries. All the pieces came in, I'm sure of it."

"Perhaps there's been some misunderstanding, sir. That's a juried show, you know." Chandler spoke in a slow, measured voice but the Santa beard muffled his words. He pulled the ear string off one side of his fake beard and left it dangling. The beard danced up and down as he talked, and Jane thought it gave him a whimsical look. But the levity seemed lost on Tony and his wife.

"I'm sorry if your submission wasn't chosen," Chandler continued. "You understand that's up to the juror's discretion. Sometimes ...."

"My painting was accepted. I've got the letter to prove it," Tony snarled. "I told that other guy! When's he coming back?" He stood on his toes and scanned the crowd, then turned to his wife. "I'm sick of this. A bunch of lackeys. They don't know what they're talking about. We need to find that other guy."

"Volunteers," Ruth Alice said. "Not lackeys. I'm sure there's been a mistake. Nobody stole your painting, Mister _____ ? Why don't I check the records and see if we can straighten this out. Let me get your name and number, and I'll ...."

"That's what he told me," Tony growled. "But I'm still waiting for him to get back to me."

"Tony, this isn't good for your blood pressure," the tiny woman said. "There's nothing we can do tonight if that other man's not here." She looked at Ruth Alice. "You're the director of this? This place?" She waved her hand toward the crowd. "How about you tell us when that other man will be back? There's no use in us going through this whole explanation over and over again. I don't know who stole my husband's painting, but it's missing, and it's high time somebody explains to us what's going on. If you can't find the painting, then it's only fair for you to compensate us for it." She opened her patent leather purse, took out a card and slapped it on Ruth Alice's palm. Then she slid her hand under Tony's arm and guided him out the door.

At the bottom of the stairs, she turned back. Her expression was as poisonous as her tone of voice. "If we don't hear something from you people by Monday, I want you to know we're calling the police."

Ruth Alice, Chandler, and Jane stood speechless for nearly a minute as they watched the couple leave. Then Ruth Alice said, "Well, that was alarming."

"I've heard you say that before," Jane said. She took a deep breath. "I believe your next statement is: 'Never a dull moment.'"

Donna padded over and picked up a bottle of wine and a plastic stemmed glass from the table. "Red as an angry visitor?" she said as she offered to pour a glass of wine for each of them.

Jane and Ruth Alice both shook their heads, but Chandler nodded and said, "Make it a full pour, would you? This little Santa needs some Christmas spirits." He exhaled. "You know, I was sure that guy was going to take a swing at me. He's beefy as a bull. I was praying he'd go for a gut punch. At least I have plenty of padding around my belly."

Jane looked at the pillow-bulge under Chandler's waist, then glanced at his face and burst out laughing. "Do you know how silly you look with that beard dangling off one ear?"

Chandler shrugged. "Just trying to keep the visitors happy."

Donna cocked her head in the direction of Tony and his wife. "I don't think you succeeded."

Jane looked at Ruth Alice. "Have you any idea what that man was upset about? A stolen painting?"

"Not a clue," Ruth Alice said. "But as soon as we get this reception cleared out, I'm going to go up to my office to try and figure it out."

"Did I hear you say something about a clue?" Pam said as she sauntered up to the table. Her hand was resting on the shoulder of a short, dapper man in a forest green shirt and red polka-dotted bowtie. Pam raised her eyebrows to signify the importance of what she was saying. "I've brought somebody for you to meet, Jane. This is Andrew James Harrison. DOCTOR Andrew James Harrison. Native of Atkinsville. Grandson of Doctor James Harrison."

Jane blinked. What was Pam getting at? Did this Doctor Harrison have some relationship with bulky Tony and his cobra of a wife?

"Doctor?" Donna asked Pam. "You mean like the Case of the deh..." She stopped herself before she uttered the word, 'deadly.' "Er, Tonsil Day? The one they used to have in the Studio Annex?"

CHAPTER SIX

On Wednesday morning, as soon as she finished feeding the cats, Jane checked the calendar in her phone:

- Choir practice, St. Ignatius Church,10:30-1
- Santa Store, AAC, 2-5

Jane was really looking forward to her stint at the Santa Store. She had signed up for one of the two volunteer slots at the check-out table. The work would be easy enough - usually, on weekdays, merely a trickle of customers visited. And whenever Jane volunteered at AAC, she ran into people she knew, so it would be as much a social event as a job.

But the real reason Jane was eager to go to AAC was curiosity. She wanted to find out what had come of the kerfuffle with that couple at the Friday night reception. Since Ruth Alice had been in meetings the whole day yesterday - while Jane's watercolor group had been painting at the center - she didn't have a chance to drop by the director's office for a casual chat. Jane didn't think it was appropriate to call Ruth Alice and ask. After all, Ruth Alice was a professional - Jane shouldn't waste the director's time with gossip.

But Jane had been musing about bulky Tony and his venomous wife since Friday night. Did he really have a painting that had been accepted into one of AAC's juried shows? Tony certainly didn't seem like the artist-type. But then again, what was the "artist-type?" Wasn't AAC a haven for older people who had always wanted to create but were too busy in their younger days with careers and kids? Did Tony's painting really get stolen? Jane had never heard about any artwork getting stolen at AAC, but that didn't mean it had never happened. Hopefully, Jane would bump into Ruth Alice while she was working at the Santa Store this afternoon, and then she could casually inquire about the incident.

At 10:10 a.m., Jane loaded into her car a box of typed programs for the annual holiday choir concert. Her choir would perform the concert twice - once at the church and a second time at the AAC holiday gala. By mutual consent, Jane always made the programs for all the choir concerts. She didn't mind; she was a whiz at both organizing and writing so it seemed like a natural fit for her to take on this task. Before her retirement, Jane had worked as a writer/editor for the university's Department of Home Economics. But preparing this year's program had been unusually challenging since nearly half of the selections were songs from around the world, and the titles were in foreign languages. After the chorus finished rehearsing, Jane planned to show the programs to the choir members and ask them to check for errors before she delivered the program to the printer.

The church was a short drive from Jane's subdivision. Rehearsal started promptly. The conductor took them nonstop through the full chorus numbers to give them a feel for the length of their upcoming performance. For Jane, singing in a group was always exhilarating. She loved contributing her voice to a unified work of art that soared to the high ceiling and bathed an audience in glorious sound. At this time of year, with the performances so close, Jane felt a tingle of excitement pervading the room.

As soon as they finished running through the full-chorus songs, the conductor talked to the group about the numbers that needed some attention. Then he brought the soloists onstage to practice their parts. The other singers sat in the pews to listen. That's when Jane passed out the typed copies of the program.

Cathy Barron walked over to the pew where Jane was sitting and whispered that her name was mistakenly spelled with only one R on the program.

"Oops, sorry," Jane said. "It's a typo. I'm glad you spotted it. I've seen your name printed on the list of Angelas so many times. I should have caught that."

Cathy smiled. "Twenty-five singers plus all these foreign song titles and composers' names. You had a lot of spelling to check. It must have been a real bugbear to put this program together. I appreciate you taking charge of it."

"Thanks," Jane said. "Actually, I enjoy it. Now that I'm retired, I'm not spending all my time editing publications for the U. So this kind of work seems like fun."

"I know what you mean," Cathy said. "When I was teaching, the last thing I wanted to do was take on more projects and deal with more personalities. But now that I'm retired, I love volunteering at AAC. It's fun to get involved with all the projects and personalities. Speaking of AAC, I was at the reception Friday night. What was all that shouting about?"

Jane shrugged. "I'm not exactly sure. Some man named Tony. Big, bulky guy. Has a tiny little wife with white hair. I never met either of them before. They said AAC lost Tony's painting. He got so mad that he actually threw a wine bottle across the hallway. It crashed into one of Donna's paintings. But it could've been a lot worse. At least it didn't crash into anybody's head."

Cathy shook her head. "I think I know who you mean. Tony Keller. He works with my husband."

"Really? You know him? I forget - what does your husband do?"

"He has that auction house and antique mini-mall," Cathy said. "The one at the corner of Route 552 and Billy Barron Road."

"I've never been out there, but I remember passing by it on the road. They auction mostly farm equipment, don't they?"

"Mostly," Cathy said. "But sometimes they get a truckload of office furniture. A store goes out of business or an estate closes. They get a lot of antiques, too. Picture frames, bottles. China. You know, collectibles. Tony runs the antique mall."

"Does he lose his temper - like that - often?"

"No, I wouldn't say that. But he has his moments," Cathy said. "Dealing with the public can sometimes be trying."

"That's for sure," Jane said. "But you'd think he'd would've learned to control himself. I mean, he really flew off the handle at the reception. Jabbing his finger at Ruth Alice. Practically attacked Chandler."

Cathy's eyebrows shot up. "Oh, dear. Next time I'm at the store, I'll ask him about what happened. If I find out anything, I'll let you know."

"Thanks," Jane said. "I'd hate for him to go around bad-mouthing AAC. He accused the art center of losing his painting."

• • •

After choir practice, Jane stopped at Christina's Cafe - down the road from AAC - for a quick lunch. She was finishing up her sweet potato fries - Christina's specialty - when her phone buzzed. She wiped the grease off her fingers and tapped the screen. Pam had sent a message:

Doc Harrison has Friday off. I'm meeting him for lunch. Christina's at noon. Can u come?

Jane smiled. Christina's was definitely the popular meet-and-eat spot in Atkinsville. She checked her calendar, then she texted Pam that she'd be there.

When Jane pulled into the lot across from the Old Gym, she saw only two or three cars. As she expected, the Santa Store wasn't going to be very busy this afternoon.

Inside, Jane greeted Roberta Roberts. She was wearing a red apron over her forest green long-sleeved sweater. Tiny red light bulbs dangled from her earlobes. Again, Jane was reminded of Mrs. Santa. "Are you finishing your shift or just starting it?" Jane asked her.

"I've been here since 11, when the store opened," Roberta said. "I signed up for back-to-back shifts."

"Oh, if I'd known," Jane said, "I would have brought you something for lunch. I just came from Christina's."

"That's so sweet. I do love that cafe. But I just finished my sandwich," Roberta said. "Anyway, you don't need to be worrying about me going hungry." She patted her tummy. "Doesn't look like I'm in danger of starving, does it?"

Jane grinned.

There were a few shoppers already wandering through the store, and two more women came in behind Jane. A well-dressed woman approached the check-out table and asked a question about the wreaths. Roberta stood up. "Let me give you a hand," she said. "I made several of the wreaths."

Jane put her pocketbook on the floor behind the table and settled herself on a folding chair. She located the cash box, a credit card swiping machine, and a pen on the table. Then she checked the pile of bags and tissue paper. Everything seemed ready for business, so Jane let her gaze meander around the room. In one corner, she saw two tall Christmas trees decorated with felted ornaments in the shape of birds, angels, and Santas, as well as Donna's popular Nessies. Next to the trees was a clothing rack with hand-stitched Christmas aprons. The far table was piled high with crocheted hats, woolen scarves, and mittens. Above the knitted goods stood a shelf of pottery - Christmas mugs, Kwanzaa candleholders, and Chanukah menorahs glazed with the Star of David. Plush lambs, hand-sewn teddy bears, and wooden dreidels bedecked stools and display counters. The scent of greenery infused the room.

Ruth Alice poked her head in the doorway and waved at Jane. "Are you here alone?" she asked.

"No, Roberta's here." Jane pointed at the back wall, where Roberta was showing off a large wreath decorated with pine cones and red and green plaid ribbon.

"When you get a minute, can you come up to the office?" Ruth Alice asked. "I've got somebody up there who wants to talk to you."

Jane raised her eyebrows.

Ruth Alice came closer and lowered her voice. "Officer Strickland," she said. "Beau Strickland. Real nice man. He's here to collect statements for the police report."

Jane grimaced. "Police report? You're kidding. That couple from the reception? They really called the police?"

Ruth Alice nodded.

Jane shook her head. "That man hurls a wine bottle into a crowd, and he has the nerve to file charges against us. What gumption! Did you tell the policeman about the bottle?"

"He knows," Ruth Alice said. "But I told him we weren't going to file charges. I think the best thing to do is let the whole thing fade away."

"Did you ever find out anything about a stolen painting?" Jane asked.

Before Ruth Alice could answer, Roberta approached the table, trailed by two shoppers. "Well, hey," Roberta said to Ruth Alice. "Have you met Cindy and her daughter Jenny? They drove in from Atlanta to shop at our store. Said they come every year."

Ruth Alice and the shoppers exchanged pleasantries while Jane totaled up their purchases. Then Ruth Alice said, "See you soon?" to Jane, and she walked out with the women.

After they left, Jane asked Roberta if she could manage the store alone for a little while. "Ruth Alice asked me to come up to her office for a few minutes," Jane explained.

"Is it about that man on Friday night?" Roberta asked.

Jane nodded.

"Wasn't that awful?" Roberta said. "Can you imagine somebody acting like that? Throwing a wine bottle with all those people around! It's a wonder nobody got hurt. I told Robert that AAC should press charges. I bet the man was drunk. What do you think?"

"Not sure. But the policeman is waiting, so I've got to hurry," Jane said as she retrieved her pocketbook from under the table. "If you get busy, just call Ruth Alice's office."

Officer Beau Strickland rose as Jane entered. Ruth Alice introduced them, and the policeman shook Jane's hand. Although he looked to be a fairly young man - Jane guessed he was maybe 35 - his handshake was hearty and confident. Strickland had a hometown air about him, with his curly blonde-brown hair, clean-shaven face, turned-up nose, and friendly smile. He was short for a man, with a trim and muscular build. Jane guessed that he'd played on his high school's baseball team. He was handsome enough to have been the school's Homecoming King.

"I won't take up too much of your time," he said, as he offered Jane one of the chairs across from Ruth Alice's desk. "I understand you're one of AAC's most valuable volunteers."

Jane beamed at Ruth Alice. "I really do love this art center," she said. "I come here to paint every Tuesday. And I try to help out whenever I can. I helped Chandler hang the show in the galleries." She waved her hand in the direction of the galleries.

"I understand you were in the hallway when Tony and Mary Keller entered the Old Gym on Friday night," he said. "Tell me what happened."

"Well, I wasn't aware of them," Jane said, "until the wine bottle crashed into Donna's painting. I'm pretty sure I've never met the Kellers before. I was showing our group's watercolor paintings to a visitor when I heard the glass shatter. That's what made me turn around." She went on to explain what she'd witnessed and - to the best of her memory - what everyone had said.

Strickland took notes on a small pad. With smiles and nods, he encouraged her to recall as many details as possible.

"I'm the one who kept track of the paintings that were juried into the show," she concluded. "There was nobody with the name Tony on the list. I'm sure I'd remember seeing it."

"I checked," Ruth Alice interjected. "He didn't submit anything for this show. But he did have a painting in Summerfest. Not this past summer - a year and a half ago. So that's when his painting was lost. Or stolen. If what he says is true."

"So, it must have happened when the previous director was here?" Jane asked.

Ruth Alice nodded. "Yes. I found the list of entries on the computer. Tony Keller's painting was selected by the Summerfest juror. It was listed NFS - not for sale."

"Did the artists sign a check-off list when they picked up their paintings? Is there any record of that?" Jane asked.

Ruth Alice checked the monitor on her laptop. "Doesn't look like the previous director kept track when the artists picked up their unsold work." She looked up and shrugged. "I don't think he was the greatest at record keeping."

Jane chuckled and looked at the policeman. "Ruth Alice is being diplomatic. Our previous director - Aiden Parson - was not organized. I wouldn't be surprised if Tony's painting really did get lost on his watch."

After a few more questions, Strickland thanked Jane for her time. "If you think of anything else, please give me a call," he said as he handed her his card. "Sometimes the most trivial detail is important."

"Will do," Jane said as she popped his card into her pocketbook. "As a matter of fact, I wrote down everything I could remember about the incident when I got home Friday night. Seems to calm me - writing notes. I've got to admit that my nerves were a little jangled after that bottle went crashing into the painting right behind me. Anyway, I'll check my notes this afternoon and see if there was anything that I forgot to tell you."

"Jane is our amateur sleuth," Ruth Alice said, grinning. "I believe the watercolor painters call you Shirley Holmes, don't they? She was at a painting retreat in the spring where a murder occurred, and she's the one who cracked the case."

The policeman looked incredulous. "A murder case? At a painting retreat?"

Jane blushed. "The retreat was at a resort where they keep thoroughbred horses. Pricey racing horses." She waved her hand back and forth as if to brush away the topic. "It's a long story. Anyway, I didn't exactly crack that case."

Ruth Alice leaned forward and raised her eyebrows. "That's not what I heard."

"Well, I guess I did help identify the murderer. In a way," Jane said. She shrugged. "I was just in the right place at the right time."

Strickland chuckled. "Well, if I ever run across a murder case in Atkinsville, I'll be sure to call you," he said. "But this is a small town. The most serious things we see here are drunk teenage drivers and roaming dogs."

"Actually, we may have a murder case at AAC," Ruth Alice said to Strickland. "You know about the skeleton that Jane found in the art closet? I never have heard the conclusion of that mystery."

Strickland looked at Jane. "So, you're the one who found that skeleton? I believe that was a child's skeleton, wasn't it? From a long time ago."

"That's what the forensic scientist speculated. But she was going to run some tests to be sure," Ruth Alice said. "I haven't seen the forensic report. Have you?"

Strickland shook his head. "No, but now you've got me intrigued. I'll follow up on it and let you know what I find out." He chuckled. "I never thought of this art center as a hotbed of crime."

"I hope that's not going to be its reputation," Ruth Alice said.

Strickland stood up. "I appreciate your speaking with me, ladies. Now, if you'll excuse me, I've got some other matters to attend to."

After he left, Jane looked at Ruth Alice. "I bet you didn't know - when you took this job - that you'd be filling in police reports."

Ruth Alice laughed. "Like I say, never a dull moment."

Jane stood up.

"Wait a minute," Ruth Alice said. "'Before you go, I have some good news for you: Your painting sold."

"The cat in the bag?"

"That's right." Ruth Alice picked up a copy of a receipt. "A woman named Susan. Susan McDaniel. She called this morning. Said she couldn't stop thinking about that painting. Has the perfect spot for it in her den."

As soon as Jane returned to the Santa Store, she blurted out the good news about her painting.

Roberta hurried out to the hallway to take a look at the painting. When she returned to the check-out table, she said, "You glued a paper bag on it. Wasn't that clever of you!"

Jane grinned. "I'm pretty thrilled that it sold," she said. "I was showing it to the woman who bought it when that man threw the bottle across the room."

"Well, there you go," Roberta said. "Maybe that's what made your painting unforgettable."

CHAPTER SEVEN

On Friday morning, Jane delivered the concert program to the printer, with all the corrections in place. She explained the format and where her black and white sketches should go. The meeting with the printer took longer than she expected, so she was running a few minutes late for her lunch meeting with Pam and the tonsil doctor's grandson.

As she drove to Christina's, Jane pondered what she'd learned about tonsillectomies. Last night, she'd Googled the "History of Tonsillectomy" and discovered that infected tonsils have been blamed for all sorts of medical woes - from hoarse throats to asthma, from polio to bedwetting. President George Washington actually died from a throat abscess caused by infected tonsils. As a result of this infamy, doctors had been removing the glands for 3,000 years. The first doctor to describe the operation lived in Rome a century before Christ. He'd used his finger to extract tonsils! Over the centuries, advances in medical know-how had improved the safety of the surgery. In the 1940s and '50s, tonsillectomies were performed frequently, reaching a peak of nearly one and half million procedures in 1959. But after Alexander Fleming discovered antibiotics, the popularity of the operation eventually waned.

As Jane pulled into the small lot in front of the cafe, she grabbed an open spot. Although it was a sunny day, it was a little too chilly for outdoor dining. Inside, she scanned the room. People were seated at most of the tables, but there was no sign of Pam. Jane spotted a man sitting alone at a table against the wall. He had on a jaunty bowtie over a dark shirt. Jane remembered that Dr. Harrison had worn a bowtie at the AAC reception.

She walked over and introduced herself. "Sorry to be late," she said as she stuck out her hand to shake his. "I don't know if you remember me from the AAC reception, Dr. Harrison. I'm Jane Roland."

"Please call me Andy." He took her hand, then gestured to the bench across from him. "This place is popular, isn't it?"

"Seems to be a favorite lunch spot," Jane said. "I love their sweet potato fries."

They exchanged small talk until Pam finally bustled in. "Oh, that dog!" Pam groaned. "Don't ask me how she managed to get her big body over the fence. She saw the neighbor's new kitten, and off she went. I thought I'd never catch her. Chased the kitten all the way down to the end of the road. Probably scared the poor little thing to death. I had to drag Tillie home, then go back and coax the kitten out of the bushes and bring her over to the neighbor's house. I didn't know if she could find her own way home, as young as she is. That kitten was probably so disoriented after Tillie ...."

Pam stopped and looked at Jane and the doctor. "I'm sorry. You didn't want to hear all that. Anyway, that's why I'm late. I guess you two have already made each other's acquaintance?"

Doctor Harrison's smile was a study in patience. "Perhaps we better go ahead and order," he said. "I need to be back at the office at two."

Jane didn't know how to begin the conversation, so she was relieved when Pam took the lead: "Like I told you on the phone, Dr. Harrison, when I was researching the history of the AAC buildings for that project with the school, that's how I learned about Tonsil Day. The kids couldn't believe that a doctor would actually come to school and perform surgery right there, in the atrium." Pam chuckled. "I mean it's a big airy space, but it's not exactly a hospital."

"Please call me Andy. Gramps told me about Tonsil Day when I was a kid." He grinned. "At first, I thought he was joking. He was a big tease, you know. But after I got into med school, he told me the story again, and he assured me it was for real." He shook his head. "Times have certainly changed."

"So, your grandfather lived to see you become a doctor," Jane said. "I bet he was very proud."

"Actually, he died while I was in med school. Said it was a family tradition."

Pam looked puzzled. "Huh? Dying is a family tradition?"

Andy laughed. "Well, now that you mention it, I guess it is. In every family. But I meant 'medicine.' Medicine is a family tradition. My dad was a gastroenterologist. He's retired now."

"And what's your specialty?" Jane asked.

"I'm an orthopedic surgeon. Medicine has changed a lot since Gramps' day. He was what they used to call a 'family doctor.'"

The conversation dwindled when their food arrived. Jane looked around as she bit into her turkey and sprouts sandwich. Each table at Christina's was one-of-a-kind. The tops of the rectangular picnic tables had been hand-painted in vivid, Crayola colors. Framed paintings by local artists decorated the walls. Everything about the place, from the chalked menu on the wall above the cash register to the wooden toys in the children's play corner, announced 'hometown' and 'locally-owned.' Even the aromas - fresh sandwich bread, deli meats, pound cake - reinforced the message. As Jane looked at the paintings, she noticed that each had a little tag with the title, artist's name, and sale price. She made a mental note to ask Christina if she'd be willing to let their AAC watercolor group display their paintings sometime.

Pam picked up the conversation when they were finishing their sandwiches. "So, I wondered if your grandfather ever had a problem - you know - at Tonsil Day. If something might have gone wrong. I'm guessing it wasn't like doing an operation in a hospital, where he had a full range of equipment in case of an emergency."

"Are you asking me if Gramps ever lost a kid on Tonsil Day?" Andy asked. He chuckled. "Not that I know of. Thank goodness. You know, a tonsillectomy is pretty routine. Why, in small towns, doctors used to perform tonsillectomies during house calls."

"I understand that tonsillectomies became much safer after 1909," Jane said. "After a doctor figured out how to seal the cut to prevent hemorrhaging."

"You're up on your medical history," Andy said. "I guess you've been doing research on tonsillectomies?"

Jane nodded.

"Do you think your grandfather would've told you about it?" Pam said. "I mean, if something did go wrong."

"Well, I can't say for sure. Gramps did regale me with all sorts of stories."

"He might have been embarrassed," Jane suggested, "if there was a problem. People like to share their successes, but nobody likes to admit their mess-ups."

Andy squinted at them. "I guess there's a reason you're so interested in tonsillectomies?" Andy said.

Jane sighed. The cat was out of the bag, or - she mused - the tonsil was out of the throat. It was time to tell Andy where their inquiry was leading. "Maybe you heard about the skeleton that we found at AAC?" Jane said.

Andy nodded.

"It was a child's skeleton. That's what the forensics expert said. I wondered if the skeleton could have had something to do with the tonsillectomies."

Andy shrugged. "I guess it's possible. You're thinking a child might have died during the procedure?" He considered before continuing. "But I would think that if a child did die, the family would have collected the remains to bury them in their church cemetery or in a family plot. Weren't the AAC buildings the old school complex? I've never heard of children being buried at a school. Unless maybe those news reports about boarding schools for native American children. I don't think we had anything horrific like that here in Atkinsville, did we?"

"Not that I know of," Pam said. "Nothing like that showed up when we did the research into the history of the AAC buildings. I guess maybe there could have been a boarding school earlier - before the Atkinsville School was built."

"How old was the skeleton?" Andy asked.

"I don't know," Jane said. "We haven't seen the report from the forensics expert."

Andy glanced at his phone, then stood. "I need to head out," he said. "But now you've got me curious. I'll ask my dad what he remembers about Tonsil Day. If there were any mishaps. If I learn anything, I'll let you know, but I don't think it's likely."

"Please understand that we're not trying to accuse your grandfather of any wrongdoing or tarnish his reputation," Jane said. "It's just so uncanny to find human bones in an art center. Especially when they were placed in the closet recently." She explained that she'd discovered the bones in the drawing studio closet when she was returning the plastic skeleton after the opening.

Andy cleared his throat. "That plastic skeleton. I was at the opening for the show," he said. "The little boy really freaked out, didn't he?"

Was it Jane's imagination, or did Andy seem relieved to shift the conversation away from Tonsil Day?

"Good thing kids don't have heart attacks," Pam said. "Or we might have had another dead body at AAC."

"Please don't remind me," Jane groaned. "I can't believe I ever thought it was a good idea to hang that skeleton in the gallery."

"Everybody makes mistakes," Andy shrugged. "Usually, they aren't fatal." He nodded goodbye and strolled out of the cafe.

Pam pushed her plate toward Jane. "Do you want some of my sweet potato fries? I'm stuffed."

Jane couldn't resist munching on a few, even though she wasn't hungry. She poured some ketchup onto Pam's plate.

"I guess we didn't learn anything from Doctor Tonsil," Pam said. "He seems like a nice enough guy. Not the type of man with skeletons in the closet. Then again, it's always the nice one that you don't suspect. In a whodunnit."

"Actually, it would be the grandfather whodunnit - not Andy," Jane said. "But I agree. Andy seems like a reasonable person. I was afraid he'd get his hackles up when we were probing his grandfather's tonsillectomy practice. He didn't seem to get ruffled. But I did think he seemed relieved when the conversation moved to plastic - not real - skeletons. What did you think?"

"Not sure," Pam said. "I thought he was getting a little bit nervous, but it was because he needed to be back in the office at 2."

Jane munched on another sweet potato fry, then pushed the plate across the table, as far away as her arm would reach. "These fries are addictive. I'm not even hungry, but I can't quit eating them." She checked the time on her phone screen. More than an hour before she'd promised to be at AAC. An idea popped into her head. "Pam, do you have anything to do this afternoon?"

"Well, ordinarily I'd have to go home and take Tillie for a walk," Pam said. "But she's gotten plenty of exercise today. Why? You have something you want to do?"

"I promised Ruth Alice that I'd start bringing home the cartons of glass dishes for the gala," Jane said. "They've all got to be run through the dishwasher. They get dusty after a year in storage." Jane glanced at the time on her screen. "But I don't need to be at AAC until after three. There's an antique mall at the corner of Route 552 and Billy Barron Road. You know the place? The man who runs it is Tony Keller. You know, Tony-throw-the-bottle-at-the-reception." She looked at Pam. "So, how would you feel about going shopping?"

CHAPTER EIGHT

For the short ride to the antique mall, they hopped into Jane's car and left Pam's car in Christina's lot. Since the lunch rush was over, nobody would mind - there was plenty of open parking around the cafe.

"What's our plan?" Pam asked as they headed toward the south end of the county. Billy Barron Road was just outside the Atkinsville town limits, in an area where pastures outnumbered people. "Are you going to ask Tony Keller about his claim that his painting was stolen? Or just pretend we're in the market for antiques and hope he doesn't recognize you?"

"I don't really have a plan," Jane said.

Pam raised her eyebrows. "You? Without a plan? Are you feeling okay?"

Jane smiled. Going to the antique mall was a spur-of-the-moment idea. "It just popped into my head," she said. "If Tony recognizes me and says something, I guess I'll ask him about his painting. But if he doesn't, I thought we'd just observe him. See what he's like. This nasty man who makes a big ugly scene and then files a police report against an art center."

"So, this is like a trip to the zoo?" Pam said. "To observe the wild animal in its habitat?"

Jane giggled. "Now you put it that way...."

"I'm just wondering if we should stop off at my house first."

"Why?" Jane asked. "Do you need to pick up something?"

"No, but if we're getting in a cage with a tiger, maybe we should bring Tillie along," Pam said. "To protect us. She wouldn't hurt a flea, but Tony the Tiger doesn't know that."

"I think we'll be safe enough," Jane said. "I doubt he'll go ballistic when he's at work."

"Well, he threw a wine bottle into a crowd at AAC," Pam said. "In an antique store, he's going to have all kinds of glassware to throw around."

A large sign by the side of the road announced their destination: Barron's Auctions and Antiques. They pulled into the dirt parking lot surrounding two buildings - a red auction barn with white trim and a long, low antique mall with a metal roof. A rustic wooden fence separated the parking lot from the buildings. The auction barn was closed, and a large sign on its side read: *"Barron's Auctions. Farm and Lawn Equipment. Check newspaper listings for auction times."*

There wasn't any activity at the antique mall, either, and it didn't look like any lights were on inside. Jane stopped the car, and they walked up the dirt path to the mall entrance. A hand-lettered sign hanging from the doorknob said the mall was closed for inventory and gave a phone number to call. Jane put her nose up to the glass on the door and shaded her eyes so she could look inside. She could see a heavyset man holding a clipboard. He glanced in her direction. Although it was hard to make out his expression with the sun behind her, Jane thought he looked angry.

Jane turned to Pam. "Do you think he can see us? It's sunny out here and it's dim in there."

"I don't know," Pam said. "Does he look like he recognizes you?"

"Can't tell. But I think he's glaring at me."

"In that case, he probably recognizes you," Pam said. "Is he coming to the door?"

"No," Jane said. "He's gone into a room. I think it's his office."

"This place is giving me a bad feeling," Pam said. "I'm glad he didn't come to the door. I don't want to be alone with a tiger. Let's get out of here."

Jane and Pam returned to the car. As they drove back to Christina's parking lot, Pam offered to help Jane with the plates for the gala.

"That'd be great," Jane said. "If you'll take home some of the boxes and run the dishes through your dishwasher, it'll make the process go much faster."

"How many people have bought tickets?" Pam asked.

"Almost 200. But most people wait 'til the last minute to get tickets. And if the Old Gym's not at capacity, they'll sell tickets at the door, too."

"What's capacity?" Pam asked.

"Five hundred."

Pam whistled. "Hmm. I should have asked before I volunteered. That's a lot of dishwashing."

They stopped at Christina's so Pam could pick up her car, then they drove up the street to AAC. Inside, Ruth Alice greeted them from her desk.

"I recruited Pam to help with washing the dishes," Jane announced.

"Good for you!" Ruth Alice said. She beamed at Jane, then at Pam. That radiant smile was the best payback, Jane thought. It made volunteers feel like purring. "You're sure you two are comfortable carrying boxes up from the tunnel? I don't want anybody getting hurt. Chandler will be here in the morning, and he can put the boxes into your cars."

"It's going to take awhile to run 500 dishes through the dishwasher," Jane said. "So, I think we need to go ahead and get started. We'll be careful on the stairs. Don't worry."

Ruth Alice handed Jane her keys.

"Any word from the forensic scientist about our skeleton?" Jane asked as they turned to leave.

"Not yet. I called and left a message. But so far, no word," Ruth Alice said.

Jane led Pam through the Central Gallery and out the back to the tunnel door. It was locked. Thank goodness, thought Jane, as she punched in the code. The less traffic going through the tunnel, the better. She didn't want any surprises greeting her from the subterranean recesses of these old buildings.

Once in the tunnel, Jane could smell the musty, damp odor from dirt floors and walls. She led Pam down the narrow stairs. The aged wood creaked with every step.

"The dishes are stored in the old bomb shelter," Jane said. "Have you ever been in that room?"

"No, I've only been in this tunnel two or three times," Pam said. "Tell you the truth, it gives me goosebumps when I have to go down here. It reminds me of an old horror movie. It even smells like one."

"Since when can you smell a movie?" Jane giggled inwardly. Pam was such a poet!

"Since the first time I ever saw a scary movie," Pam said. "When I sneaked out to the movies with my best friend and didn't tell my mom where we were going and saw *Godzilla*. That would be, like, 60 years ago. I felt like the monster was reaching out of the screen to grab me. I could smell his putrid breath. I really could."

The lock on the bomb shelter was the old-fashioned kind, with a key. Jane tried three of the keys on Ruth Alice's ring before she found the one that opened the deadbolt. The door stuck on the lumpy dirt floor when she tried to push it. She leaned her shoulder and hip against it and rammed as hard as she could. When it was three-quarters open, she stuck her hand inside and felt around for the light switch.

"This is the creepiest of the creep," Pam said as she looked around the old bomb shelter. "Like a cave. It's no wonder our caveman ancestors took to building structures. Who'd want to go to sleep in a place like this?"

Cardboard boxes were stacked on the ground and on wooden shelves. Jane stuck the ring of keys in her pocket and started opening the tops of the boxes. She slid four cartons aside after peeking inside and seeing they were full of the small snack plates with slots to hold the stems of wineglasses - rather than tableware for a sit-down meal. She made a mental note to mark the outside of the boxes with the word 'Gala' so it would be easier in the future to figure out which boxes held which types of dishes.

"Looks like someone came down here and dusted the shelves," Jane said. "But not the tops of the boxes with the Gala plates. Amazing how dusty they've gotten in a year. In a room where there's barely any traffic."

"I think these shelves are wedged - not screwed - into the dirt walls," Pam said. "I guess there's no way to screw them in. I wonder if anybody's ever inspected this place? I bet it would be condemned."

"A lovely thought," Jane said. "Here, this one isn't too heavy." Jane handed Pam one of the cartons. "Can you manage it?"

"No problem," Pam said as she took the carton. "I was the wheelchair Mom, remember?"

Jane remembered the stories that Pam had told about her life as a young mom. Pam's son had muscular dystrophy and used a wheelchair. For almost 20 years, Pam had loaded his wheelchair into the trunk of her car and carried her son in and out. She'd been determined to give her boy a full life with regular outings and the activities that every child enjoys. Eventually, tragically, Pam had lost the boy, but she hadn't lost the muscles that she'd developed. Nor had she lost her poetic perspective on joy which shines all the brighter because it's highlighted by grief.

With her box in hand, Pam turned and started toward the door. Suddenly, she sneezed. A great whopper of a sneeze, which brought tears to her eyes. Then she sneezed again. And a third time.

"Allergies?" Jane asked.

"I guess," Pam said. She sneezed again. "All this dust. Plus, it's moldy down here. And damp, and .... Achoo!" Pam stepped back and leaned against the shelves to steady herself.

The fifth sneeze did it. It made the wall come tumbling down. Literally.

CHAPTER NINE

Jane opened her eyes, but in the intense darkness, she couldn't see a thing. Her body seemed to be sprawled on something hard and bumpy. Stony. Damp. A mound of rocky soil? She was lying in an awkward position, and she could feel a heavy object pressing against her foot. She touched it. It was smooth and long and flat. A board? Was she wedged under a structural beam? Was it safe to move? Holding her breath, she shifted, ever so slightly. The board moved. She shifted more, and it slid off. She took a deep breath and coughed. The air seemed to be full of dirt. She could taste it. Her mouth was gritty. She flexed her fingers, wiggled her torso, stretched her legs. No pain. But maybe she was in shock, and the shock was blocking the pain? Where was she, anyway? Why was it so dark?

She coughed again, and her memory began to reassemble. The old bomb shelter! They'd been in the bomb shelter to get the dishes for the gala. Pam was with her. Had a bomb gone off? No, don't be ridiculous, Jane scolded herself. This was a bomb shelter built decades ago. AAC used it for storage. There weren't any bombs - they weren't at war.

So, what happened? Panicking, Jane's mind groped for an explanation. Had the tunnel caved in? Were they trapped down here? Where was Pam?

"Pam?" Jane said in a whisper. Then she asked herself: Why am I whispering?

"Pam," she repeated in what should have been her normal speaking voice but came out garbled. She spit. Ugh, her mouth was full of grit. She tried to operate her voice again. "Where are you? Pam?"

A groan.

"Pam! Can you hear me? Is anything broken?"

"Not sure."

"Oh, no. Better not move," Jane said. "What do you think is broken?"

"Probably every single dish in this box," Pam said.

Pam started coughing. "Tell me again why we don't use disposable plates for the gala?" Pam said. More coughing. "You know, they make really elegant disposable plates nowadays. Some of them are even biodegradable."

Jane could hear Pam stirring. Was it safe to move, Jane wondered? Terror washed over her. Were they in danger of a cave-in?

"Better stay still," Jane urged. "The wall must have given way. I don't know if we're in danger of a cave-in."

"Darn it!" Pam said.

"Are you hurt?" Jane asked. "Try not to move anything, okay? Until we know that none of your bones are broken."

"I left my phone in the car," Pam groaned. "When am I going to learn that the dumb thing only works in an emergency if I take it with me?" She sneezed. One, two, three sneezes.

The sneezing triggered Jane's memory. "Oh, no, don't sneeze!" Jane yelped. "That's what got us into this mess."

"It's not so easy to stop a sneeze, you know," Pam said. She sniffled, then coughed. "Well? Do you have your phone?"

Phone - yes, phone! What am I thinking? Jane took a deep breath and told herself to breathe. Calm down. Was her phone still in her pocket? Trying not to move too much lest something vital shifted and they got buried alive, Jane's fingers fumbled along her clothing. She located her waistband, ran her fingers down her slacks and patted her pocket. There it is - my phone! Immense relief flooded through Jane's every vein. She forced herself to pause and take another deep breath, then she slid out her phone, brought it to her face, and pushed the button. The screen lit up! Would she get reception down here? She pushed the green phone icon, and hit 911. It rang! An operator's voice filled the void. Jane explained their whereabouts and situation. The operator asked if she was alone. Were they injured? Jane told her they seemed to be okay. Nobody was in terrible pain. They could breathe. The operator said help was on the way and instructed Jane to remain where she was and keep the line open.

Now, Jane turned the lit screen toward Pam, who was sitting in a pocket of rubble in front of what looked like a gaping cavern. In the dim light, Jane could see Pam's face, which was smudged with dirt. Her hair looked dusty. But Pam seemed oddly comfortable with her situation. She flashed a lopsided grin, raised one of her arms, and wiggled her fingers in Jane's direction, which made Jane think of a toddler in a mud puddle. Clearly, Pam was not one to lose her cool in an emergency.

Suddenly, Jane remembered the flashlight app on her phone, and she clicked it on. She shined it on Pam, who grinned and waved again.

"That's bright," Pam said. "These smart phones are wonderful, aren't they? Only you have to remember to take them with you. Just promise me you're not going to take a photo and post it on Facebook. I can imagine the comments. 'Dirty old lady sneezes and brings down the walls of Jericho.'"

Jane chuckled, in spite of their predicament. "You really don't get rattled in a crisis, do you?"

"This? A crisis?" Pam gestured around the room. Then she covered her face with two hands to suppress a sneeze. "Compared to running after a little boy who decides to do wheelies on his wheelchair down a steep hill, this is a piece of cake." She looked around. "No, I take that back. This is a mudpie."

Jane shook her head. Life teaches all kinds of lessons, she mused. Pam's experiences with her son had bestowed calm and perspective. Jane couldn't imagine anybody volunteering to experience suffering or grief in order to learn from it. But, no doubt, difficult experiences were learning labs - granting a PhD in the most important lessons of the world.

"Are you still there?" said the voice of the emergency operator on Jane's phone.

"Yes."

"The emergency team is entering the building," said the operator. "They'll descend into the tunnel as soon as they assess the stability of the structure. Remain where you are - they will come to you."

Turning the flashlight beam in various directions, Jane began to inspect their surroundings. The ceiling looked completely intact, and the walls on three sides of the old bomb shelter seemed like they were undamaged. No big cracks or holes. Jane's back was starting to cramp, and she judged it was safe to sit up. But when she pushed her left foot on the ground to heave herself up, she felt a stabbing pain in her ankle.

"Yow - my ankle!" Jane cried. "I think it may be broken."

"Paramedics are on the way," said the operator.

"Oh, dear. Is the pain very bad?" Pam asked.

"Only when I try to put weight on it."

Jane shined the flashlight at the door to the tunnel. It was shut. But Jane was sure they'd left the door open behind them because the door was so hard to push. A terrible thought clamped down on Jane's frayed nerves: Had somebody followed them into the tunnel, exploded a device, and shut them in this room?

"Pam," Jane said, "do you remember if we shut the door after we came in here?"

"We didn't shut it," Pam said. "I'm sure. It was so hard to get it open, remember?"

"But it's shut now," Jane said. "Look. Do you think somebody ....? Do you think maybe someone threw an explosive in here and then slammed the door?"

"I think maybe you've been reading too many mystery books," Pam said. "Your imagination is running amok. Don't you see this big mountain of rubble in the middle of this room? The weight of all this stuff is what pushed the door closed. That's what 'dunnit.'"

Jane shined her flashlight on the mound of rubble that lay between her and Pam. Boards and boxes were jumbled in with reddish-brown clods of dirt. And some other long, boxy, wooden objects were jutting out of the pile, too. Jane couldn't quite make out what they were.

But if she had to guess, she'd say they looked like rough-hewn caskets.

CHAPTER TEN

The opening notes of a minuet transported Jane to a moonlit sky, where she floated through gauzy curtains spun of silk and cotton candy. Then, reality waltzed into her brain and rammed her awake: That's my phone - not an orchestra! She'd reset her phone settings to play the minuet whenever she got a text message.

She opened her eyes. Definitely no moonlit night, she thought, as she squinted at the bright sun pouring through her window. What time is it, she wondered? What day is this?

Whew, she thought, I must have been deep asleep. What did I do yesterday that made me so tired? Slowly, memories materialized. The tunnel and the bomb shelter. Collapsed wall. Injured ankle. Emergency room. Painkillers. That was it - the doctor in the emergency room had given her painkillers, and she'd taken one before she went to bed, last night.

Minuet began to play again. Jane picked up her reading glasses and looked at her phone, which was charging on her bedside table. The text was from Betsy:

Do u need anything? Groceries? Wine? Coming at noon. Bringing lunch.

Lotus trailed after Jane as she hobbled to the bathroom. Tylenol, she decided was a safer bet than another painkiller. She fished around the medicine cabinet and located the bottle of Tylenol. Lotus, who seemed to sense how difficult it was for Jane to get around without the use of her left ankle, somehow communicated this insight to Levi when they got downstairs to the kitchen. Both cats moderated their usual ear-piercing chorus of complaints regarding their morning hunger. After fortifying the cats, Jane fortified herself with toast and tea. Then she hobbled back upstairs and ran herself a hot bath. The doctor's instructions were to alternate ice and heat on her injury, keep her weight off her ankle, and take it easy. After surviving a cave-in, Jane figured she'd earned that prescription.

While she waited for Betsy to arrive, Jane dozed in a sunbeam on the living room couch, her left leg elevated on a footstool and an ice bag draped over her ankle. With Lotus warming her lap, Levi heating her thigh, and the sun shining on her shoulder, Jane hardly noticed the chill invading her foot.

At the first clonk of Betsy's sensible shoes on the landing, Levi vanished. Jane watched Lotus's ears swivel toward the intruder's sound. The brown tip of the cat's tail began to twitch. But the female Siamese seemed determined to maintain her rightful position on Jane's lap - even if Jane did display a deplorable lack of manners by moving her lap as she turned to face the door.

Letting herself in, Betsy boomed, "How's the ankle?" She used the hearty voice that she'd developed when she was a professional occupational therapist greeting a patient. At the sound of Betsy's voice, Lotus skittered out of the room.

"Not too bad. I've been taking Tylenol today."

"Pam said you have an appointment with an orthopedist?" Betsy carried an armful of bags into the kitchen, then came back into the living room and removed her coat.

"Tomorrow," Jane said. "The doctor in the emergency room said I needed to show my x-rays to an orthopedic specialist. It's kind of ironic, actually. I'm going to see Andy."

Betsy looked puzzled. "Andy?"

"Andy Harrison. Orthopedics is his specialty," Jane explained. "You know - his grandfather was the doctor who did Tonsil Day in the Studio Annex."

"I didn't realize he was an orthopedics doc," Betsy said. "Have you ever been to him before?"

"No. The first time I met him was at AAC. On the night that man went ballistic at the reception. Then Pam arranged for us to have lunch with him at Christina's. Yesterday, although it seems like weeks ago. Before the walls came tumbling down."

"Tell me again how that happened," Betsy said as she sat down. "When I called Pam, all she said was she sneezed. I mean, if a sneeze caused a cave-in, it must have been a helluva sneeze."

Jane giggled. "It was a helluva sneeze. Whenever Pam does something, she puts her whole self into it. Even so, I doubt if her sneeze was the reason the wall collapsed. It must have been weakened already."

"Weakened? How?" Betsy asked. "Just from years of mold and damp? I wonder if that whole tunnel is safe. Personally, I think it should be condemned. Has it ever been inspected?"

Jane shrugged. "I don't know. I guess it'll get inspected now. I've been wondering if the foundations of the AAC buildings are safe. If the tunnel collapsed...." Jane stopped mid-sentence as the doorbell rang. Her eyebrows raised in an unspoken question, Jane looked at Betsy.

"It's open," Betsy called toward the door. She explained to Jane, "I forgot to tell you that I invited Ruth Alice to join us for lunch."

Ruth Alice entered, beaming brighter than the sunbeam. She was holding a large bouquet of flowers wrapped in a sheet of clear plastic and an equally large box of chocolates wrapped in gold foil. "I brought you some happy medicine," she said as she handed Jane the chocolates. "How're you feeling?"

"Not too bad. I've got an appointment with an orthopedic doc tomorrow. Andy Harrison. You know him?"

Ruth Alice nodded. "Nice guy. He and his wife helped set up the reception for the Halloween show." She sighed. "The show that nobody could come see because it was surrounded by yellow police tape."

"Here," Betsy said and took the bouquet from Ruth Alice. "I'll find a vase and get our lunch. Is it okay if we eat on trays in here, Jane? That way, you can keep your leg elevated." Betsy scurried off to the kitchen.

"Sure, that's fine," Jane called before turning to Ruth Alice. "It's so sweet of you to come over and bring me flowers and chocolates, Ruth

Alice." She opened the chocolate box and selected a dark piece with white frosting stripes. "After yesterday, I've decided to commit to the philosophy that 'life is short; eat dessert first.' Want one?"

Ruth Alice grinned and chose a piece. As she chewed, she called to Betsy, "Thanks for calling me. I'm loving the company. My office feels lonesome when I'm the only one in the building." She slipped off her nubby woolen cardigan and plopped into the padded armchair across from the couch. "Did you hear what the building inspector ...."

Betsy poked her head in from the kitchen. "Talk louder, so I can hear you," she said. "We were just talking about whether the AAC buildings are unsafe. Since their foundation is undercut by that tunnel."

"The buildings are safe, thank goodness," Ruth Alice. "Fortunately, they were built in the old days, when people didn't worry about conserving resources. Those floors are thick, and the foundation is solid."

"Well, that's a relief," Jane said. "I mean it's nice to conserve resources and all, but it's more important to build buildings that are safe for people to walk through."

"What about the tunnel?" Betsy called from the kitchen. "Are they going to condemn the tunnel?"

Ruth Alice shook her head. "Evidently, the tunnel is sturdy. Except for the bomb shelter. It was added later - decades after the original tunnel was dug. The bomb shelter just happened to butt up against a cemetery."

"Huh?" Jane and Betsy exclaimed in chorus as Betsy came flying out of the kitchen.

"A cemetery?" Betsy said. "What do you mean? For the school? Like those Native American schools where they buried kids that had been abused?"

"No, no," Ruth Alice said. "Nothing to do with the school. It was a cemetery from a really long time ago. Probably, some settlers built it. The forensic anthropologist from the university said it was probably on someone's farmland. She guessed that's where the skeleton of that child came from."

"I don't understand," Jane said. "You mean the skeleton in the art closet? The one we found?"

Ruth Alice nodded. "Yeah. The anthropologist will have to do some more analysis. To see if the time period matches. But she thinks the skeleton from the closet came from this old cemetery that abutted the bomb shelter. There was only a few feet of dirt between the wall of the bomb shelter and the burial vault. If they'd kept digging the bomb shelter - made it just a little longer - they would have poked through and exposed the caskets."

Jane could feel her eyes bulging. "So, those were caskets that I saw in all that rubble? Wooden caskets? They were really crude looking." Jane tried to picture how many caskets she'd seen in the rubble. There were at least three, she remembered. She wished she'd had the foresight to take a photo with her phone.

"Yes, they were caskets," Ruth Alice said. "The anthropologist said there were at least five caskets in that vault. Some of them must have been stacked, maybe on shelves that leaned against the back wall of the bomb shelter. She was going to try and determine who the people were. Look up the county records to see who owned that land. Do DNA analysis. Eventually the authorities will have to find a place to reinter the remains."

"Wow, that's really interesting," Betsy said as she carried in a tray holding a plate of sandwiches, a basket of chips, plates, and glasses. After putting the tray on the coffee table, she went back to get the vase of flowers and a pitcher of water. "Y'all want water?"

"That's fine," Ruth Alice said. "Can I help you carry anything else?"

"No, this is it," Betsy said. "Chicken salad or egg salad?"

"How about a half sandwich of each?" Jane said.

"Ruth Alice?"

"I'm starving. They both sound good. How about if I take the other half of each?"

Betsy handed a plate to Jane and poured some water into a glass for her. Then she slid the tray toward Ruth Alice. "Tell us more about what the anthropologist said. Did she ever figure out how old the kid was - the one whose skeleton we found?"

"Well, that's interesting," Ruth Alice said. "I read her report this morning. At least, I read some of her report - the parts I could understand. The skeleton did belong to a child, like she suspected. But there's no way to tell whether the child was a boy or girl. Only that the child died before puberty, probably around the age of 10 or 12."

"Really," Jane said. "I thought they could tell all kinds of things from bones."

"They can. But with kids, they look for things that happen at regular stages, like when teeth erupt and when cartilage changes into bone. They determine gender from the pubic bones after a kid reaches puberty. In adults, there are skull differences, too. Like females usually have pointier chins, and males have bigger brow ridges."

"That's intriguing," Betsy said. "I love forensic science, don't you? So, all we know is the skeleton belonged to a child who was maybe 11. And I guess the DNA will tell whether the child was related to the other people in those caskets. What about cause of death? Does the anthropologist think it was a disease? Maybe the kid's whole family died of smallpox or something."

"Wait a minute," Jane said. "All these details about the child's skeleton are fascinating. But the real mystery is how a skeleton from a cemetery long buried managed to get into the art closet in the Studio Annex."

"It was Halloween," Betsy said. "That's when ghosts and skeletons roam the streets."

Jane rolled her eyes. "Well, this child was too old - literally - to go Trick or Treating. Seriously, how could a skeleton escape from a casket and suddenly appear on a closet shelf?"

"If you think that's mysterious, wait until you hear the rest," Ruth Alice said.

Jane stared at Ruth Alice. "What do you mean? The rest?"

"When they were putting the caskets into the van to take them to the lab, one of the caskets was heavier than the rest. Way heavier." Ruth Alice paused and looked at Jane.

"So, you mean one of the caskets contained the bones of an adult," Betsy suggested. "And the others held the bones of children?"

Ruth Alice shook her head.

Jane gasped as she realized what Ruth Alice was hinting. "Oh, no!" Jane stared at Ruth Alice. "You mean - one of the caskets held the remains of a dead body? Not just bones."

CHAPTER ELEVEN

Jane's appointment with Doctor Harrison was at 10 a.m. She figured she'd need at least two hours to get herself up, dressed, and ready, since she had to be careful to avoid putting any weight on her left foot.

Betsy had a work meeting this morning, so she'd taken it upon herself to call Grace and ask her to drive Jane to the doctor's office. When Jane found out, she'd objected - the emergency room doctor told Jane that, since the injury was to her left ankle, she could drive as long as she wasn't on heavy-duty painkillers. But Betsy had insisted, and Jane didn't have the energy to argue. Jane had long ago decided that if she was constructing a crossword puzzle about her friends, she'd choose "insistent" as the perfect clue for Betsy. Grace, on the other hand, would be the solution to the clue, "gentle." If Jane had to have a driver, she was relieved it was going to be Grace.

Grace arrived at 9:20 and helped Jane navigate her crutches along the cement walkway to the car and into the passenger seat. On the ride, they chatted about Ed Walker, the attorney that Grace had recently begun to date.

"I enjoy his company, I really do," Grace said. "He's knowledgeable about art and so many other things. He enjoys attending events at AAC. We have a lot in common. But after that experience last spring, I'm keeping things very low key. Ed may be charming and witty, but so was Arthur. I guarantee that I learned my lesson. And then some."

Jane nodded. Arthur was a painter who had been in their watercolor retreat at Gardens and Horses Resort. He was a real charmer, and he'd shown a romantic interest in Grace. "Well, you know what they say about jumping back in the saddle after a fall," Jane said

Grace smiled. "Very apt metaphor!"

Andy's office was located in a bustling complex of medical offices. Expecting parking to be difficult, Grace dropped Jane off at the front of the building while she drove around the lot in search of a space.

Jane had just finished registering on the computerized kiosk when Grace joined her in the lobby. They found seats in the waiting area.

"If you wouldn't mind, I'd like to go in with you," Grace said. "I always think it's a good idea to have a second set of ears at a doctor's appointment. It's just so easy to miss something important. They throw so many medical terms at you."

"Sure. That's fine." Jane smiled. "But admit it: The real reason you want to go in is curiosity. You want to check out the grandson of the famous Tonsil Doctor."

Grace grinned. "Guilty as charged. But I really do think it's a good idea to have a companion when you're listening to medical advice."

At the doorway, a nurse called, "Mrs. Roland."

"That's Ms, not Mrs.," Jane said as she hobbled through the doorway. "I'm not married." She smiled to reassure the nurse that she wasn't offended by the mistake. "Is it okay if my friend Grace comes with me?"

The nurse nodded. On the way to an examining room, Jane was measured and weighed. In the examining room, the nurse took her temperature, recorded her blood pressure, said the doctor would be in soon, and closed the door.

It was a standard doctor's office, except for a large, framed painting on the wall. "Look at this," Jane said to Grace. "I'm pretty sure it's an original - not a print. And the frame is really fancy."

"You said this doctor is an active member of AAC, didn't you?" Grace asked.

Before Jane could answer, Andy opened the door. "I am an active member of AAC," he said, "and very proud of it." He was wearing a red and green striped bowtie over a bright red buttoned-down shirt, with a white doctor's coat open in the front. Striding into the room, he flashed a sparkling smile and shook Grace's hand as Jane introduced them. "I believe I've seen your paintings in the hall outside the Santa store?"

Grace nodded and smiled. "Yes, you have. Thanks for noticing."

"And I believe you're a friend of Ed Walker?" Andy asked.

"I am," Grace said. "How do you know Ed?"

Andy nodded. "Ed and I go way back. We went to school together. Say hello to him for me."

"I will do that. I'm guessing you're a fan of the Santa store," Grace said. She indicated his bowtie.

Andy touched the bowtie, and it began to pulsate with light. "I'm like a big kid at Christmas," he said. He touched his bowtie again to make the pulsating stop.

"Seems you've brought your passion for art into your medical practice, too," Jane said, pointing at the framed painting. "Are you the painter?"

"Me? Oh, no. I used to paint, but, these days, my art interest is limited to appreciation." Andy looked at the painting. "This is an original oil, an old one. It's signed, but I haven't had any luck finding information about the artist. From the subject matter, I'm guessing he was American. I did some research on the age of the frame, though. It seems like the painting was placed into that frame when it was still wet. I found traces of paint around the inside edges. If that's the original frame, I'm pretty sure the artist was 19th century."

"Well, I'm impressed," Grace said. "You must be quite the expert in art history."

Andy nodded. "My undergrad major. Gramps talked me into going to med school. He said that following my passion for art was a prescription for financial ruin." Andy shrugged.

Setting his laptop on a small metal desk, Andy rolled a chair over to the examining table where Jane was seated. "Now, let's have a look at this ankle. Go ahead and take off your shoe and sock. I reviewed your x-rays from the emergency room. The report says you were injured in a cave-in?" He picked up Jane's left foot and moved it up and down. Then he asked her to wiggle her toes. "Tell me if this hurts."

"Only when you twisted the foot," Jane said. "Believe it or not, it really was a cave-in. I know it sounds crazy, but the wall in that old bomb shelter - in the tunnel below AAC - collapsed. I was down there with Pam. We were getting the dishes for the gala - to take them home and run them through the dishwasher. You know, to get the dust off. You've been down there, in the old bomb shelter, haven't you?"

Andy had rolled his chair over to the computer desk and was typing some information into Jane's chart.

"Ruth Alice says you helped with the Halloween Show reception," Jane continued. "So, you must have seen that room. It's where AAC stores all the glassware."

Andy looked up. "Yes, I do know where you mean. First time I was down there was a couple of weeks ago, when I carried the snack plates upstairs for my wife. She was in charge of food for the reception. She and Cathy Barron."

"I used to teach with Cathy," Grace said. "She's such a sweetheart."

"Her husband has that auction barn and antique mall," Jane said. "I bet that's where you found that painting?"

Andy smiled. "You're quite the sleuth, aren't you! Yes, Sam sometimes gets lots from estate sales. He knows I'm a fan of old paintings. Especially when they have elaborate frames."

"He calls you when he gets a new shipment of paintings?" Jane said.

Andy laughed. "He does. He's a smart businessman. He's also a good friend."

"You know the man who works for Sam? At the antique mall?" Jane asked. "Tony Keller."

Andy nodded.

"He's the man who made a big scene at the opening of the Santa store," Jane said. "Claims AAC lost his painting. You know anything about that?"

"I heard about some man making a scene, but I didn't know it was Tony. He has a stubborn side, that's for sure," Andy said. He glanced at the clock on the wall. "Getting back to your ankle, the x-rays show a hairline fracture in your lateral malleolus. That's the bottom of your fibula. Your ankle bone. The good news is it should heal on its own - no surgery. But I want to keep an eye on it. I'm going to order a few more x-rays - we can do them here, we've got the equipment - just to be sure the other bones are okay." He took a small pad out of his coat pocket and scribbled on the first sheet, then handed it to Jane. "This is for the pain. Take them as needed."

Jane took the paper. "I don't know if I'll fill this. The doctor in the ER gave me some pain pills. I took one, and it really knocked me out. I've been taking Tylenol, instead, and that seems to take care of it."

"That's fine," Andy said. "You may want to switch to Ibuprofen, instead. To reduce the swelling. Just be sure you have something in your stomach when you take it." He looked at the crutches that Jane had propped against the wall. "He told you to keep your weight off the foot?"

Jane nodded. "And he said to keep my foot up as much as I can, and apply ice alternating with heat."

"Good," Andy said. "I'm going to have the nurse bring you a boot. You can use that if the crutches are too difficult to maneuver." He rolled back to the laptop and typed. "I guess something hit your leg when the wall collapsed?"

"Must have," Jane said. "The cave-in knocked me out. When I came to, there was a board on top of my foot. Looked like one of the shelf boards. That's probably what hit my ankle."

"Must have been frightening," Andy said. "Did they check you for a concussion at the emergency room?"

Jane nodded.

"Well, I'm glad you got off with just a hairline fracture. How about your friend Pam?"

"She's fine. Rattled, of course, but no injuries. The glassware, however, is a total loss. Pam says it's just as well. AAC should be using disposable plates. They may be harder on the environment, but they're a lot easier on the volunteers."

Andy smiled. "A little less elegance but a lot more convenience. And I think you can get compostable dinnerware these days. Any idea what caused the collapse?"

"Well, the immediate cause was a sneeze," Jane said.

"A sneeze?" Andy blinked.

Jane chuckled. "I'm kidding. Pam's allergies kicked up - it's so dusty and moldy down there. She kept sneezing. She was leaning against the shelves, and suddenly, the wall came tumbling down. It must have been weakened already."

"Hmm." Andy cocked his head. "Any idea how it might have gotten weakened?"

"Evidently, the bomb shelter was right up against an old cemetery," Jane explained. "Are you a gambler, Andy?"

Andy seemed startled. "I guess I've done my share of gambling," he said.

Jane shrugged. "So what are the odds that an old cemetery would back up to an old bomb shelter. Under a small town art center."

Andy nodded thoughtfully. "I'd have to say they were pretty slim."

"Ruth Alice said the wall was thin to start with - only a foot or two of dirt." Jane shook her head. "And if that isn't weird enough, get this: When the wall collapsed, some old caskets fell into the room."

"Oh, my! Who would have expected that?" Andy said.

"And one of the caskets contained a body - not just a skeleton," Jane said.

Andy's eyes opened wide. "A body? Like a recent body?"

Jane nodded.

Andy gasped. "How, I mean, when would a body...? Do they know who? I'm flabbergasted. What did the police say about this?"

"I haven't heard any more details," Jane said. "Ruth Alice says the police are investigating, and she'll know more in a few days. But she has gotten the report from the building inspector. The rest of the tunnel - and the AAC buildings - are safe. Thank goodness."

Andy stood. "Well, I'm glad to hear the art center is okay." He walked to the door and turned as he said, "I'll send the nurse to take you to x-ray. If I see any other problems, I'll call you." He opened the door.

"Um, one more thing," Jane said.

Andy stopped.

"The gala's coming up, and I sing in the choir," Jane said. "Is it okay if I stand for an hour or so? I can probably sit during part of the rehearsals, but it would be awkward to sit during the actual performance. I promise I'll be careful not to put any weight on my ankle."

Andy said, "Shouldn't be any problem." He chuckled as he added, "Just don't break a leg."

Jane cocked her head. "Huh?"

"Isn't that what they say in show business? Break a leg?" Andy grinned. "Seems like you've already done that."

CHAPTER TWELVE

Jane sat at her kitchen table, her left leg elevated on the chair beside her, a mug of hot tea wafting comfy aromas around her. Lotus, who was perched on Jane's lap, batted at crumbs from Jane's toasted and buttered bagel.

Morning sun flooded the kitchen countertop from ceiling-high windows. The rays bathed an African violet blooming in a pretty handmade pot. Its purple flowers seemed in harmony with the blue and purple glazes on the pot. Jane had purchased it from her favorite potter at AAC's last Summerfest show. In spite of her injured ankle and the recent disturbing events at the art center, Jane felt warm and secure, like the violet. She was looking forward to the weeks ahead, to her choir performance and AAC's gala, as well as the Christmas holidays.

Her phone played a minuet, its ring-tone. The sound startled Lotus, who jumped off and skittered into the living room. Just past the open doorway, Levi ambushed her and pounced. As the cats rolled into a pulsing pincushion, Jane picked up the phone. AAC's number was displayed on the screen.

"Hi, Jane, how's your ankle?" Ruth Alice's voice sounded as comforting as the mug of Earl Grey warming Jane's fingertips.

"It's okay. I saw an orthopedic doc yesterday. Andy Harrison. He said it's a hairline fracture, and it should heal on its own."

"That's good news," Ruth Alice said. "Hey, listen, are you busy this morning? Beau Strickland - you remember him? The policeman. He called. They got the report from the medical examiner. Beau wants to talk to both of us about it. I told him about your ankle, and he said he'd be glad to come to your house if it's more convenient."

Jane glanced around. The place seemed presentable enough. Her watercolor group was coming over at lunchtime, but the morning was free. "That's fine," she said.

"Okay, we'll be there in a few."

Jane gulped down the rest of her tea and prepared an ice bag for her ankle. When the doorbell rang, she opened the front door to a bear hug from Ruth Alice. Officer Strickland pulled up behind Ruth Alice's car in the driveway. He opened the window on the driver's side of his squad car and waved.

"Okay to park here?" he called.

"Sure," Jane answered.

"Let's talk in the living room," Jane said, as he came inside. She hobbled over to the sofa and put her leg up on a footstool. "I'm supposed to apply ice to my ankle as often as I can."

After replying to their questions about her injury and offering her guests a drink, Jane settled back to hear what the policeman had to say.

Strickland looked at them and swallowed. "Well, we got the report from the coroner. It's something of a surprise." He took a deep breath. "I wanted to talk with both of you before the news is released to the media. This is a small town, and an unusual situation. I'm expecting a big splash. Rumors flying everywhere." He paused.

Ruth Alice leaned forward. "So, the body in the casket.... Was it somebody we know?"

Strickland nodded. "Aiden Parson."

After what seemed like several minutes of shocked silence, Jane realized that her mouth was hanging open. She shut it. The clap of her teeth sounded as loud as a cannon firing inside her head.

Ruth Alice leaned forward. "Aiden Parson? You mean, the former director of AAC? He was in the casket?"

"How did he get in the casket?" Jane asked. "Wasn't it on the other side of a wall?"

"There are many unanswered questions in this investigation," Strickland said. "That's why I wanted to talk with both of you. You knew Aiden?"

"I knew of him," Ruth Alice said. "He was gone before I took the job." She stammered. "Er, left. I don't know if he was still alive. But he wasn't at AAC. At least, I never saw him there. He didn't stay on to train me or anything."

"As I understand it," Jane began, "Aiden just stopped showing up, one day. People - I guess board members, Chandler, some others - they tried to call him. To see if he was sick or had gotten hurt or whatever. But he never answered his phone." Jane shrugged. "He was a pretty useless director, overall. A do-nothing. I'm not sure if it made any difference at AAC when Aiden went missing. He did absolutely nothing when he was working as the director."

"But nobody reported him as a missing person to the police?" Strickland asked. "He just disappeared? What - y'all hired a new director, and that was all? Weren't you worried about what would happen if Mr. Parson showed back up at work?"

"Well, it wasn't as cold-blooded as you're making it seem," Jane said. "I know Chandler tried to call him. Several times. And other people wrote him emails. I was told that the board members were making efforts to contact him. They called the people who had given Aiden references from his previous position. For weeks - as I understand it - people tried to reach him. He didn't respond to calls, texts, emails. Nothing. It was like he'd dropped off the face of the Earth."

"That seems to be what happened," Strickland. "Only he didn't drop into the earth by himself. Somebody must have put him there. And covered it up."

"You're saying Aiden was murdered?" Ruth Alice gasped.

Strickland didn't reply.

"Well, that's a bit alarming," Ruth Alice said. "I mean, it's a lot alarming. I realize people get passionate about art. But murder? When I became the director, I certainly heard a lot of complaints about Aiden's job performance. About how his negligence was destroying the art center. But I wouldn't think anybody hated him enough to actually kill the man."

"Who made these complaints?" Strickland asked.

Ruth Alice turned to Jane, then said, "I don't know. Everybody? The members of the board, for sure. Chandler, the man who hangs the shows. Volunteers. The Angelas."

Strickland pulled out a pad and pen from his pocket. "Can you be more specific? Which board members? Which volunteers? What is Angela's last name?"

Jane grinned. "The Angelas are a sort of club. Women who support the art center by making crafts to sell. They sponsor receptions, do fundraisers. Things like that. The group calls itself the Art Angelas."

"Can you remember which of these women complained about Parson?"

Jane strained to remember specific conversations involving Aiden. "I remember talking with Cathy Barron once. We were saying how incompetent Aiden was," Jane said. "Mind you, I'm not accusing Cathy. She's just in the same choir group as I am, so we see each other a lot, and she's active at AAC - like I am. But she's certainly not a murderer. Cathy's one of the Angelas."

Jane sorted through her memories of Aiden. The former director was a tall, slim - almost gangly - man. Large hands, big feet. His face always reminded Jane of a horse - long and narrow, with a prominent forehead and big ears. He had grayish brown hair, and he always wore jeans, even to dressy events. His most distinctive feature was his outsized handlebar mustache. He was obviously vain about the mustache. He must have kept it dyed, since it was deep brown - almost black - with no strands of the gray that flecked his hair and eyebrows. While the mustache was unusual and clearly meant to garner attention, it went along with Aiden's overall look. He affected a Western style of dress: shirts with mother-of-pearl snaps, string ties, belts with heavy silver buckles, cowboy boots, and chunky turquoise rings. Jane remembered asking Aiden if he'd grown up out West, but he'd shrugged off the question.

Of course, Jane mused, lots of artists used their bodies as their canvasses. They got tattoos or piercings or wore quirky attire. She knew one sculptor who had a map of the world tattooed on his shaved head. Many of the younger women artists at the center dyed their hair bright, unnatural colors, like purple or green. Jane knew one artist who liked to spray paint red stripes and gold stars on his shoes. Even among Jane's circle of older painters, some of the women affected a particular style. Like Donna's berets. Or Pam's colorful silk scarves.

"I can't remember who else I talked with," Jane continued. "The women in my painting group used to share stories about things Aiden did - or, more likely, didn't do - while we were painting. He was always getting to work late, so we had to wait outside until he arrived and unlocked the building. He would forget to order the postcards announcing our exhibits, so we had to email our friends and post our own notices on Facebook to let people know about our events. Aiden Parson was lazy and irresponsible. Everybody thought so. It wasn't like any one particular person was out to get him."

"Who hired this man?" Strickland asked. "Who was responsible for overseeing his job?"

Jane and Ruth Alice looked at each other. "The board of directors, I guess," Ruth Alice said. "They make the center's policies and manage things. That's who hired me. They sent out a call for applications. To art departments, museum organizations - places like that. Then a search committee chose applicants to interview. I'm sure they used the same process when they hired Aiden."

"Who was on the search committee?" Strickland asked.

"Ed Walker was the head of the search committee that hired me," Ruth Alice said. "He's the attorney for the board. But I doubt if the same people were on the search committee that hired Aiden. He was director for what? Barely two years."

"You have a list of search committee members - recent and farther back?" Strickland said. "And board members?"

"I can get you all that information," Ruth Alice said. "Can I send you an email when I get back to the office?"

Strickland nodded. "But what I really want to know is if somebody really hated Parson. Had a reason to want him out of the picture."

That made Jane chuckle. "Bit of a pun, eh? Out of the picture," Jane said.

Strickland didn't react, but Ruth Alice smiled.

Jane strained for ideas that might help the investigation. "Well, I guess I do remember one person who was really mad at Aiden. You remember there was that man, Tony Keller? The one who was yelling at the reception for the Santa Store? He claimed AAC lost his painting. He was angry enough to throw a bottle across a crowded room," she said. "That's pretty violent. I don't know if he was angry enough to murder the man."

Strickland scribbled something on his pad. "If I remember, his wife - Mary, I think her name was - said the director had stopped answering their phone calls." Strickland looked at Jane and then at Ruth Alice. "I guess she was referring to Mr. Parson?"

Jane nodded. "Did you find Aiden's cell phone with his body?" Jane asked.

Strickland shook his head. "Not yet. But we're still working our way through the bomb shelter and cemetery vault. There's a lot of dirt to sift through."

"Tell me about it!" Jane said. "How about Aiden's house? I think he lived way out in the country somewhere. He was always saying that's why he was late - because he lived so far out. Didn't he have a dog?" Jane frowned. "When I helped with one of the receptions, he said he had to get home to feed his dog. That's the excuse he gave for why he couldn't stay and help with cleaning up. The man just up and left all the volunteers to deal with it." Jane rolled her eyes. "Aiden was a piece of work, he really was."

"We've been out to his double-wide," Strickland said. "And spoken to the neighbors. One of them said the dog kept coming round looking for food. That was back in June. The neighbor's got the dog, now. Big old shepherd. Says it eats twice as much as their three little chihuahuas, combined. They were planning to send Parson a bill for the food. That's if he ever showed back up again."

"But you didn't find any clues about Parson's disappearance?" Jane asked.

Strickland shrugged.

"No signs of a struggle? No blood?" Jane asked.

"Nope," Strickland said.

"Have you looked at his financials?" Jane asked. "We're a mostly-volunteer art center. Aiden was director, but he probably didn't make a lot of money." Jane looked at Ruth Alice. "I guess you know about the director's salary. It seems like AAC is always hurting for funds."

"That's a good idea," Strickland said. "I'll check his bank accounts, credit cards. See if he owed anybody money. Had any bad spending habits."

Jane smiled. "Follow the money trail. That's what they always say in detective stories."

Strickland returned her smile. "That's why they call you Shirley Holmes, right? Because you're clever at solving murder mysteries."

Blushing, Jane said, "I guess I'm like Tupperware."

Ruth Alice cocked her head. "Huh? What's Tupperware got to do with it?"

"You know the old saying about Tupperware - that its reputation precedes it." Jane shrugged.

"I thought its reputation was you had to burp it," Ruth Alice said. "Like a baby."

Jane giggled. "I guess that's another part of its reputation. But seriously," Jane said, "I don't deserve a reputation as a sleuth. The only time I've been around a murder case was at that watercolor retreat in spring. And it was just luck that I happened upon the clue that solved the mystery."

"I heard it was a lot more than luck," Ruth Alice said. "I heard you took detailed notes. You even did research."

Jane nodded. "I guess I'm guilty on both counts. I'm an obsessive note taker. It calms me when I'm in a tense situation. But, in the end, it was Pam's dog that solved that case. For me, it was really just a matter of luck. Being in the right place at the critical time."

"Well, if luck strikes again, you be sure and call me," Strickland said.

As the policeman stood up, Jane noticed how he moved with the effortless energy of a young man.

At the door, Strickland smiled at Jane and said, "And if you decide to take some notes about Aiden Parson, I'd be interested to see what you come up with, ma'am."

CHAPTER THIRTEEN

Donna was the first to arrive for the painters' lunch. "I know I'm early," she told Jane as she let herself in. "Bill dropped me off on the way to his appointment."

Donna closed the front door and pulled three bottles of wine - one white and two red - out of her painting bag. "This is for what ails you," she said. "Actually, for what ails all of us." She grinned. "Well, look at you with your laptop! Sitting on the couch, your foot up. I guess this is what they call, 'working from home?'"

Jane smiled, "Guess so," she said. The news about Aiden was on the tip of her tongue. But she decided she should restrain herself until all the painters arrived, and she could share the information with everyone at the same time.

"I'm gonna go put these in the kitchen," Donna said, walking across the living room. "I guess we'll eat in there. How's your ankle, Jane?"

As Jane was telling Donna about Andy's diagnosis, Betsy bustled in the front door.

"I got four different kinds of sub sandwiches," Betsy announced as she marched through the living room into the kitchen. "Smoked turkey, ham and cheese, cold cuts, and tuna. I had them slice each sub into fourths so we can mix and match. I didn't know what kind of bread everybody likes, so I got Italian bread on all of them."

The door opened again. "We're here!" Maisie announced. She held the door ajar so Grace could edge in. Grace smiled a greeting at Jane as she carried her large glass bowl of fruit salad into the kitchen.

"I brought some pickles that Win made from our cukes, last summer," Maisie said. She put down her bag of painting supplies and pulled out two glass jars. "This one's dill, and this is bread and butter. The bread and butter ones are so good."

As Donna returned to the living room, she said, "Mmm, I love sweet pickles."

"Help!" Pam called from the porch.

Donna rushed to open the front door, and Pam stumbled in, her painting bag over her shoulder and a large, floppy cardboard box from the local pastry shop teetering in her hands.

"Fresh baked brownies," Pam announced. "From that little bake shop downtown. They were pulling them out of the oven when I got there. And they're still warm. Can you smell them?"

When lunch was arrayed on the kitchen table, Betsy helped Jane hobble in. All of them couldn't fit around Jane's small table, so Pam and Maisie settled on stools at the counter.

As soon as they loaded their plates, Jane announced: "I've got news!"

"About your ankle?" Pam said, her mouth full of sandwich. "How is it? You went to see Doctor Tonsil, yesterday. Right?"

"Yes," Jane said. "He said it's a hairline fracture. Should heal without surgery." She took a breath prior to changing the subject, but Pam jumped in, again.

"That's good to hear," Pam said. "What did you think of Andy as a bone doc?"

"He seemed fine," Jane answered, then opened her mouth to make her announcement: "You'll never guess...." she began.

But Grace had already begun speaking. "I thought he seemed very competent," Grace said. "Also very personable. You talked with him when you met him for lunch at Christina's, Pam. Didn't you think...."

Jane couldn't hold in her newsflash for another second. She slapped her hand on the table and blurted out: "I've got news!"

Everybody looked at her.

"About the dead body in the casket," Jane announced. "It was Aiden!"

Silence.

"Aiden? You don't mean the director, Aiden?" Betsy said.

"Yes, I do mean Aiden, the director - well, former director - of AAC," Jane said. "Aiden Parson. His body was in the casket."

"How did he get into the casket?" Pam said. "It was on the other side of that wall."

"How does anybody's body get into a casket?" Betsy said. "Somebody must have put him there. Are you saying that somebody killed Aiden? Then hid his body in the casket and rebuilt the wall?"

"Maybe that's why the wall collapsed," Pam said.

"Of course, that's why the wall collapsed," Maisie said. She began to giggle. "You didn't really think it was your sneeze that did it, did you?"

Pam shrugged. "I don't know. I have powerful sneezes."

"I'm beginning to feel a little woozy," Donna said. "All this talk about a dead body."

"Here, Donna, put your head down," Grace said as she cleared away a space on the table for Donna to rest her head.

All the painters knew that Donna, who was the oldest member of their group, had fainting spells - that's why she no longer drove a car. Although Donna claimed her fainting was caused by her high blood pressure, she also seemed to get dizzy whenever she heard upsetting news.

"I think you're just shook up by the news about Aiden. Take deep breaths." Grace said. "Relax."

"That's what I'm trying to do," Donna said. "Some wine would help."

"I'm on it," said Pam, who was sitting closest to the fridge. "I think we could all use a glass of wine to help us digest this disturbing news."

While Pam opened the bottles, Maisie reached for the stemmed glasses in the glass-fronted cabinet. As soon as everybody had a few sips of wine, Jane continued. She explained that Officer Beau Strickland had visited, that morning, with Ruth Alice. "Strickland wanted to know if there was somebody at AAC who might have wanted to murder Aiden."

"Everybody at AAC wanted to murder Aiden," Betsy said. "The man nearly wrecked our art center."

"You know, he did irritate lots of people," Grace said. "And I can't say I liked the man. But I'm sorry to hear he's dead. I feel a little guilty about assuming, all these months, that he just upped and left AAC in the lurch. Without giving us any notice."

"I agree," Betsy said. "The man was an awful director, but he didn't deserve to die. Incompetence shouldn't be a death sentence."

"Maybe it wasn't somebody at AAC. Maybe it was one of Aiden's drinking buddies," Maisie suggested.

Everybody looked at Maisie. "Aiden had drinking buddies?" Jane asked. "Why do you say that?"

Maisie shrugged. "Well, I guess I don't know about buddies. Win saw him one night at the Cowboy Cafe. Win likes to go there when they have a live band. I forget the name of the group that was playing."

"Was Aiden with somebody?" Jane asked.

"No," Maisie said. "Win said he was alone. And that he was soused."

"You think Aiden had a drinking problem?" Jane asked.

Maisie shrugged, again. "Well, duh. I mean, the man's mustache always smelled like he was marinating it in whiskey." She took a sip of her wine. "I'm guessing that he didn't use liquor as his styling gel. So, the smell must have come from drinking. Heavy drinking."

"He did smell like booze," Donna said. She raised her head. "I had an uncle out in the country that smelled like that. Like booze was oozing out of his sweat glands."

"Yuck," Pam said. "I remember that Aiden did have a - shall we say - 'distinctive' odor. I assumed it was because he was a light bather. But it might've been because he was a heavy drinker."

Jane looked around the room. "Did any of you ever see Aiden out drinking? Or out with anybody? At a movie, maybe, or a restaurant? Did Win see him at the Cowboy Cafe any other time?"

"I don't know," Maisie said. "I'll ask him."

Jane looked around, but nobody else offered any information about Aiden's companions or social life. "Hmm. I guess we better stick to what we remember at AAC," she said. "Did you ever talk to anyone at AAC about Aiden? Someone who was really really angry with him? The policeman is compiling a list of people to interview."

"Chandler used to get really mad at him," Maisie said. "Remember that time Chandler quit? That was because of Aiden."

"I remember when Chandler quit," Jane said. "But I never knew why. Someone on the board talked Chandler into staying. Isn't that right?"

"Yes. The board actually voted to give Chandler a raise to convince him to stay. But we almost lost him because of Aiden," Maisie said.

"I remember hearing about that," Pam said. "But I never knew what upset Chandler so much. He's always struck me as an easygoing guy."

"Chandler's salary was automatically deposited in his bank account," Maisie explained. "For two months in a row, the AAC account didn't have sufficient funds to pay him, and Chandler's gas bill - and a bunch of other bills that were automatically deducted - didn't get paid. Chandler didn't realize the problem until the gas company turned off his heat. It was a big mess. He had a bunch of late fees and penalties to straighten out."

"The art center didn't have enough funds to pay Chandler?" Pam said, "I knew things had gotten bad when Aiden was director, but I didn't know they were that bad."

"Aiden really screwed things up," Maisie said. "Chandler was always having to pick up the pieces. I don't know where Aiden worked before he was hired by AAC, but somebody should have warned us about what a poor manager he was."

"Ed knew Aiden from Boulder," Grace said. "That's how Aiden heard about our search for a director - Ed was on the search committee. Aiden was an art instructor at the University of Colorado when Ed was getting his law degree. Then Aiden had a job at a museum. I think he came with good references."

"Is that why Aiden always dressed like Wyatt Earp?" Donna asked. "Because he was from Colorado?"

"I thought Wyatt Earp was from Kansas," Pam said.

"Oh. Do they wear cowboy boots in Kansas?" Donna asked.

Maisie started giggling. "Some people wear cowboy boots in Georgia," she said. "Aiden did."

"Maybe that's why he smelled so sweaty," Pam said. "I mean, who wears boots in Georgia? Especially during the summer. It's too hot."

Jane rolled her eyes. "It seems we've wandered off the topic. I doubt if Aiden's body odor was the reason that somebody killed him."

"You're right, it might not have had anything to do with the art center," Betsy said.

"His cowboy boots didn't have anything to do with the art center?" Pam said.

Jane rolled her eyes, again. The wine is probably not helping this discussion, she thought. "I think we should forget the man's boots and body odor," she said. "You know, this is serious - a man was murdered. All of us spend a lot of time around AAC, and something we remember could be important for solving this case. Officer Strickland really needs input."

"You think we're being frivolous," Grace said to Jane. "And you're right, as usual. It's just that this news is so, I don't know ... hard to believe. It's so sudden. Shocking."

"Bizarre," added Betsy. "That's what it is. Bizarre. We're grasping for comic relief, Jane. But you're right. We need to calm down. Think. Analyze." She looked around the room. "So, what do we know about Aiden? Besides the fact that he was incompetent."

"And lazy," Maisie added.

"And smelly," Donna piped up.

Betsy frowned. "I really don't know anything about him as a person. He pretty much kept his private life to himself, that was my impression." She looked at Grace. "But you said Ed knew him out in Colorado?"

"Yes, but they weren't close friends or anything," Grace said. "Ed talked like they'd been casual acquaintances. Bumped into each other at the faculty center. That sort of thing."

"I'm sure Ed will get interviewed," Jane said. "Strickland said he was going to contact the people on the search committee. Ruth Alice was going to give him a list. Board members, too," Jane said. She bit her lip. "It is odd. Now that I think about it, I don't know anything about Aiden's personal life. Was he ever married? Did he date? I don't recall seeing him with a companion at any of the events at the art center."

"Wait a minute," Betsy said. She held up her pointer finger. "He said something about a wife, once. I remember, now. I was picking up a form in the office, and Aiden was talking to Chandler in the hall. There was a really large watercolor of a nude - a rather buxom nude - and Chandler was struggling to hang it. It had a heavy frame, and it was a big painting. Chandler asked Aiden to help him lift it, and Aiden made a comment about how that could have been a portrait of his wife - too much and too hard to deal with."

"That was a pretty tasteless remark, wasn't it?" Grace said.

"I thought so," Betsy said. "I didn't pursue the conversation."

"So, it sounds like he was married once," Jane said. "And maybe there was a disagreeable divorce. Anything else? Did he have children?"

"I never heard him say anything about children," Pam said. "But he did have a brother, I know that. Remember when my brother broke his leg skiing, and I had to fly out to help him? Well, Aiden heard me talking, and he said something about his brother. How he needed his help a lot. He had some medical condition. Something serious, I don't remember him saying what it was. Anyway, I think he said the brother lived out West. In Texas maybe. Near a museum of Western art."

"That's in Gulch," Maisie said. "Win did a program at that museum when he was on the faculty of that summer teaching program in Texas."

"Maybe Aiden had an association with that museum?" Betsy suggested. "I wonder if that's the museum where he worked before AAC hired him. Was his specialty Western art? He sure dressed the part."

"Come to think of it, Aiden didn't have any of his own work on display in his office," Jane said. "Was he a painter? A sculptor? What?"

"If he had a brother, I'm wondering if anybody contacted him? After Aiden stopped showing up at AAC," Grace said. "You'd think the brother would have wondered what happened to Aiden. And he would have called AAC to ask about him, or something. Unless he's too ill. Or has cognitive issues."

Jane nodded. "That's a good point. I'll be sure and mention the brother to Strickland," she said.

After cleaning up lunch, the painters spread out in the kitchen and dining room to paint. Betsy and Pam brought in portable easels and set them up in the living room. Jane asked Grace to help her pull an easel over to the couch so she could put her leg up on the ottoman while she painted.

Last time they painted, Jane had started a portrait of Lotus curled up in a sunbeam on the foot of her bed. After sketching the cat, she'd laid a wash of soft tones of cobalt and rose over the background. She wanted to suggest contentment, relaxation - a gentle subject luxuriating in a safe, sunny spot.

But after the news about Aiden, Jane didn't feel like she could capture those emotions - not today. She felt unsettled, tense, worried. Something sinister was lurking around the edges of her safe and sunny world. Jane pulled out a fresh sheet of watercolor paper and started sketching a stormy sea.

CHAPTER FOURTEEN

As soon as her watercolor group left, Jane spread open her notebook to take some notes about Aiden. She began by listing suspects:

Tony + Mary Keller
Chandler

Perhaps she should include Ed Walker, too? Jane hesitated. Ed had invited Aiden to apply for the director's job, and he must have felt embarrassed about his candidate's dismal job performance. But embarrassment wasn't much of a motive for murder. She decided against listing Ed as a suspect. Besides, Strickland said he was going to interview AAC's board of directors, as well as the search committee that hired Aiden. Ed was on both, so the police would definitely talk to him.

That left Jane with a very short list of suspects. Maybe she was making the wrong assumption by starting with people at AAC?

Searching for inspiration, Jane's eyes flitted around the room. Her painting of the stormy sea was on her easel. It reminded her that a single gust of wind could blow up on an otherwise unremarkable day. All it took was one unfortunate moment - a sudden blast of rage, a short scuffle. Aiden's death might have nothing to do with AAC. For that matter, it might have nothing to do with the man's incompetence, his past, or his drinking habits. People were killed all the time without good reason. Death could be caused by an armed robbery, random gang violence, a hit and run traffic incident. Even an innocent accident - like a tumble from the roof when cleaning gutters - might be covered up by a person who feared the consequences of a police investigation.

But to break down a wall and bury a body in an ancient cemetery vault .... Now, that took premeditation, Jane thought. And knowledge. The killer must have known about the old bomb shelter in the tunnel. Since the bomb shelter was kept locked, the killer must have had access to the keys. At some point, he or she must have discovered that a dirt wall separated the bomb shelter from a cemetery vault. So the culprit would have to be somebody very familiar with AAC, somebody who had a reason to access the old bomb shelter. Who could that be? Chandler?

Jane pictured the AAC show curator: Chandler was a slim man, medium height, boyish build. Not particularly muscular, but he was active and agile. He could hang a show by himself, and that required climbing on ladders as well as hefting heavy sculptures. But Jane couldn't imagine Chandler killing somebody. He was such a cheerful, good-natured guy. True, he'd gotten annoyed with Aiden's mismanagement and temporarily quit. Jane frowned. Could that have been the sudden squall at sea that capsized the boat? But the more Jane tried to imagine Chandler killing Aiden, the more unlikely it seemed. No, she just couldn't picture Chandler hurting anybody.

What about one of the volunteers? Maybe a volunteer had discovered the burial vault while retrieving supplies from the bomb shelter. Maybe, while shifting a heavy box, the person had knocked a chink out of the wall. Then he or she might have shined a flashlight through the hole and spotted the caskets on the other side of the wall. Jane frowned. That seemed pretty far-fetched. If a volunteer had discovered the cemetery, surely that person would tell the director or Chandler about it. How many people would discover a hidden cemetery and keep it secret? How many people would conceal such a discovery in hopes of using it - at some time in the future - to dispose of a dead body?

As she sat and pondered, Jane realized there was a missing chink in her information. How did Aiden die? Jane had been so thunderstruck when she heard the former director was the body in the casket that she'd completely forgotten to ask about the cause of his death.

Just then, Jane's ringtone - the minuet - began to play. It occurred to her that her ringtone was an appropriate soundtrack for a British murder mystery. That thought put a grin on her face as she answered.

The call was from Pam. "I was just thinking about Aiden," Pam said. "You know, we got so caught up in body odors and cowboy boots, we never asked you how he died."

"I was just thinking that same thought," Jane said. "I actually don't know how he died. The policeman never said, and I was so shocked when I learned that it was Aiden, I didn't think to ask."

"Do you think the police know the cause of death?" Pam asked.

"I guess so," Jane said. "Wouldn't that be the first thing they'd determine?"

"Yeah, I would think so," Pam said. "Well, maybe you should call that policeman? You said you were going to let him know that Aiden had a brother. While you're on the phone, you could ask the cause of death. If we knew how Aiden was killed, it might help us figure out the killer. Say the cause of death was a fist fight, it would tell us the killer was somebody strong. Probably a man. But anybody - even a child - could slip poison into somebody's whiskey."

"Good point," Jane said. "Although I doubt if a child did the deed. You know, Pam, I think you're really getting into this murder mystery stuff. Didn't Sherlock have a sidekick? Dr. Watson, I think his name was."

Pam giggled. "Okay, if your nickname is Shirley Holmes, you can call me Pamson."

"Deal, Pamson," Jane said. "I'm going to give Strickland a call, right now."

"If you find out anything, let me know, Shirley."

"Will do, Pamson."

As Jane disconnected, another call was lighting up her screen. It was Grace.

"Hey, Jane," Grace said, "I hope I'm not disturbing you?"

"Nope, I'm just sitting here on the sofa," Jane said.

"Good, I was hoping it wasn't too tiring for you, today - the lunch, then having all of us painting the whole afternoon."

"I am a bit tired. But I'm glad y'all came," Jane said. "I enjoyed the company."

"I'm so glad. Well, I won't keep you too long. You remember, I gave Donna a ride home from your house today?" Grace said. "Well, she asked me to come in and take a look at the painting she finished the other day. Bill was there, and we told him about Aiden. He asked us how Aiden was killed. But neither of us could remember what you said about that."

Jane chuckled. "Pam just called and asked me the same question - about the cause of death. But Strickland never told me. I was too dumbstruck to ask when I found out it was Aiden. So, I'm going to call and ask, right now."

"Well, it's certainly understandable that you were taken aback by the news. I can't get it out of my head," Grace said. "All these months have gone by, and we thought Aiden had just disappeared. Derelict of his duties. It's all so ... I don't know. Horrifying."

"I agree," Jane said. "But let me hang up and see if I can get hold of Strickland before he goes off duty."

"Okay," Grace said. "If it's not too much bother, I'd love to know what you find out."

As Jane disconnected, she noticed that a text message had come in. Jane rolled her eyes when she saw it was from Betsy. Before opening the message, Jane guessed what it was about ... and her guess was correct.

What was cause of death? Betsy wrote.

Jane typed: Dunno. Will call police n ask.

Before Jane could send her message, Betsy sent a second message:

Neighbor here for supper. Told her about Aiden. BTW is it a secret?

Not any more, Jane thought. Since Betsy had already told her neighbor, her question was rather like asking somebody, 'Are you sleeping?'

Jane replied: Police didn't say. Maybe don't tell anyone else.

Jane switched to her phone's dial pad to call the Atkinsville Police Department. But Betsy's next text came through before Jane could finish entering the phone number.

Already told Sarah from Angelas. She called before supper. Should I call back n tell her to keep it secret? Might be too late. She plays bridge tonight.

Jane took a deep breath and wrote back: I will ask police if confidential.

Ok. Let me know, Betsy wrote.

Jane finished typing in the number of the police department as fast as she could - before any other call or text could come through. A receptionist at the police station picked up, and Jane asked to speak to Officer Beau Strickland. The receptionist transferred the call, but Strickland didn't answer, so Jane left him a voice message about Aiden's brother. She concluded with a request: "When you have a minute, please give me a call."

Jane hadn't set the phone down before the minuet played again. This is getting ridiculous, she thought. When she looked at the caller's photo and discovered it was Cathy Barron - not any of the painters in her group - Jane gave a sigh of relief.

"Hi, Cathy," Jane answered.

Cathy inquired about Jane's ankle, then she asked if Jane was planning to attend choir rehearsal in the morning. "I wondered if you needed a ride?" she asked.

"That's really thoughtful of you," Jane said. "Actually, it's my left ankle, so the doctor said I can drive." Jane hesitated. "But I don't know if I feel comfortable driving, just yet. So, yes, I'd appreciate a ride."

Cathy said she'd come by in the morning at 9 a.m. to pick her up. Jane was considering whether to tell Cathy the news about Aiden, but another call was coming through. It was, as Jane anticipated, Maisie - the only member of her group who hadn't followed up on their afternoon conversation. So Jane told Cathy she had to run. "See you in the morning," she said as she hung up. "And thanks again."

Switching to Maisie's call, Jane said, "Well, what took you so long?"

"Huh? What do you mean?" Maisie asked.

"To call. Everybody else in the group has already asked me how he died."

94

"Oh," Maisie said. "That's not why I'm calling. But now that you mention it, how did he die?"

"I don't know," Jane said. "I forgot to ask the policeman. But I've just put a call in to him. And I'll let all of you know when I find out."

"Thanks," Maisie said.

"So?"

"So what?" Maisie asked.

"So, why are you calling?" Jane said.

"I have some information," Maisie said. "I told Win about Aiden. It turns out, Win knew him better than I realized. They both liked the same bands. Aiden liked Country and Western, and Win does, too."

"So they saw each other at bars?" Jane asked.

"And coffeehouses. Couple of times, they ate supper together. Win says Aiden definitely had a drinking problem. And, just like we figured, he had a nasty divorce. Said his ex was always harping at him about money."

"That's interesting," Jane said. "I'll tell Strickland about that. But I don't know how Aiden's ex-wife could have been the killer. Has she ever been to AAC? I don't remember seeing a woman with him."

"I don't think Aiden's ex lives around here," Maisie said. "Win thought maybe she moved someplace after they split."

After they hung up, Jane wrote down all the info she needed to remember to share with Strickland:

- *Aiden was divorced. Where does his ex live? Has she been contacted?*
- *Aiden had a brother with a medical problem. He needed Aiden's help. Where does he live? Has he been contacted?*
- *Aiden had a drinking problem.*

Jane analyzed this information. She knew AAC didn't pay big bucks to its director, since the center was always strapped for cash. If Aiden had worked as a college teacher and at a museum in his previous jobs, he probably hadn't amassed much of a bank account. And his drinking habit must have cost him plenty. So, unless he had inherited money, Aiden must have been strapped for funds. Perhaps financial pressures pushed him into associating with dangerous people?

Jane stood up and stretched. She hobbled into the kitchen to refresh her ice pack. Her ankle was beginning to ache. Grace was probably right - the long day had really worn her out. Checking the locks on her doors, she decided to turn out the living room lights and head for her bedroom. This would be a good night to turn in early, she decided. Maybe watch a classic movie in bed. As Lotus jumped onto the foot of the bed, Jane heard her minuet ringtone again. She reached for her phone and saw it was a spam call, so she silenced the ringer. But the minuet kept dancing through her mind. Jane pulled her covers up to her neck, and had a fleeting image of a group of women dancing a minuet in a classical painting. The women were barefoot, wearing old-fashioned white robes. They were weaving through clipped hedges among the ruins of Grecian marble columns. Jane shut her eyes.

In her dream, the faces of the dancers transformed into the women in her watercolor group. The women swayed and twirled, holding their paintbrushes like long cigarette holders in a Gilded Age poster. Donna glided by, and Jane watched a sky-blue beret bouncing on her white cloud of hair. Then Maisie swirled into view. She caught Jane's eye and began to giggle. Her laughter became a snort, and suddenly Pam's dog leaped up and caught a butterfly. As each painter trailed in and out to the graceful music of the minuet, she whispered a secret. From lipsticked lips to pink seashell ears, the secrets rustled and churned. Jane strained to hear the words, but they merged into a susurration, a chorus of soft insect sounds. Jane put out her hand to tap Grace's shoulder, but, instead, she felt Betsy brush by. Betsy was waltzing with Aiden, and he had a handlebar mustache, cowboy boots, and silver spurs. He twirled Betsy around, and they danced into a dark, gaping tunnel. Before Jane could stop them, they went whirling, whirling....

CHAPTER FIFTEEN

Jane woke at 5 a.m. and rolled over, but she couldn't go back to sleep.

Probably because I went to bed so early, she thought. Well, I might as well get up. No telling how long it will take to get ready for rehearsal, since I have to be careful not to put weight on my foot.

She hobbled into the shower, then took her time getting dressed. She went down the carpeted stairs one step at a time. In the kitchen, she hopped around to feed the cats and get some breakfast for herself. As she scanned the newspaper headlines at her kitchen table, she elevated her leg and applied an ice pack to her ankle.

A text from Betsy popped onto her phone screen. Any news?

Jane began to type a reply, then decided to send the same message to all the painters in her watercolor group: Have not heard from Strickland. Left message. Have choir practice. She hoped that would discourage calls or texts for at least a few hours.

Cathy arrived a little late, and she seemed flustered as she helped Jane negotiate the walkway with her crutches. "Sam's car wouldn't start," Cathy said. "I had to drop him off at the auction barn. That's why I'm running late."

"Oh, you should have called me," Jane said. "I could've driven myself. My ankle isn't hurting right now. I'm going to have to learn to get around by myself sometime. It may be the better part of a month before I can put weight on it."

"It's no trouble to pick you up," Cathy said. "I just hate for us to be late for rehearsal."

At the church, it seemed like every choir member wanted to know what had happened to Jane's ankle. She must have told the tale of the collapsed wall and the burial vault at least a dozen times. But she didn't mention Aiden. If she brought that up, she was sure there'd be a zillion questions, and they'd never get started rehearsing.

The choir director seemed a little stressed by the late start. It didn't help that he'd searched all over the church for something that Jane could use as a makeshift stool to elevate her leg while she sang. He wanted her to sing in her usual position in the pews, so the voices would balance and blend. But the space between pews was too narrow for a regular folding chair. In the end, one of the choir members located a toddler-sized chair in the nursery and was able to squeeze it in between the pews.

It was past noon before they finished their run-through. Cathy checked her phone as soon as they were back in the car. "Sam left a message," she told Jane. "He needs for me to pick him up, and bring him to the car place. His car is ready - it was the battery." Cathy looked at Jane. "Sam's got a meeting in Atlanta, and he's going to be late getting there. I know you're probably worn out, but do you think you'll be okay if I take him to get his car before I bring you home?"

Jane tried to put a convincing smile on her face as she said, "Sure, no problem." But, in truth, her ankle was throbbing. During rehearsal, Jane had felt awkward about sitting while the rest of the singers stood, so she'd spent more time on her feet than she should have. She longed to get home and apply some ice to her ankle.

When they pulled into the parking lot to pick up Sam, he was waiting by the fence in front of the auction barn. Jane had met Cathy's husband at several AAC openings, but she'd never spent much time talking with him. He was a tall man - at least a head taller than his wife - and he looked fit, as if he worked out at a gym. Today, he was wearing a sport jacket over a white, button-down shirt. He smiled a greeting and hopped in the back seat of the car.

"Hi, Jane. How are you doing? Cathy told me about the cave-in," Sam said, "and your broken ankle."

"It's not completely broken," Jane explained. "The doctor said it's a hairline fracture. It should heal without surgery."

"Well, that's good," Sam said. "Any idea about why that wall would have collapsed?"

"Pam - you know, Pam Gerald, from my watercolor group? - thought it was her sneezing." Jane giggled. "All the mold and dust in that tunnel. But I doubt her sneezing had much to do with it. I think it was only a matter of time. The bomb shelter abutted an old cemetery. Evidently, there wasn't much wall between them. "

"I didn't know there was a cemetery, there," Cathy said. "Was there a church back there, once?"

"No, it was probably a family cemetery," Jane explained. "On a farmer's land. I guess that was pretty common, back then."

"So, they found coffins in the burial vault?" Sam asked.

Jane paused and bit the inside of her lip. Should she share the news about Aiden? Strickland hadn't told her that it was confidential. And, as soon as the newspaper picked up the story, everybody would find out. She glanced at Sam, who seemed puzzled by her long pause. "Yes," she said, in answer to his question. "It really was a burial vault. Stacked with caskets."

"Ooh, how creepy! I always avoid going anywhere near that tunnel," Cathy said.

Sam grinned. "Yes, I know."

Cathy glanced at Jane. "I made Sam carry up the dishes when I was in charge of the reception," she said. "I don't know why AAC stores them in that awful room."

"Well, they won't do it anymore," Jane said.

"Are they going to wall off the bomb shelter?" Sam asked.

"I don't know about that," Jane said. "But the dishes are pretty much a total loss. I think they threw all the boxes in the dumpster."

"Hurray!" Cathy said. "I never understood why they didn't use paper plates for the receptions." Cathy pulled her car into the parking lot of the dealership and drove around to the side that faced the service center. "I think I see your car, Sam." She steered toward a chain-link fence that surrounded the back of the lot.

"Something else they learned when the wall caved in," Jane said, "is that the cemetery contained a recent body. Not just the remains of the farmer's family from a century ago."

"A recent body?" Cathy exclaimed. "What do you mean?"

"You remember the former director? Aiden Parson?" Jane said. "His body was in one of the caskets."

Cathy turned to Jane, a look of horror on her face. "You mean.... He's dead? How could Aiden's body be in that old cemetery? Didn't you say there was a wall between the cemetery and the bomb shelter?"

"Yes, there was," Jane said. "It's a mystery. Somebody must have killed Aiden and tried to conceal the body in that old cemetery."

Cathy opened her mouth and sucked in air. "Well, I never liked the man, it's true. But I certainly never wished him dead. He was in over his head at AAC."

Jane grimaced. "I guess you meant that as a pun? That he was 'in over his head?'"

Cathy looked puzzled. "Huh?"

"She meant that he was in over his head - because he was buried under the earth," Sam explained. "Get it?"

"Oh, now I get it," Cathy said. She giggled. "No, I'm not that clever. What I meant was that Aiden wasn't suited to the job of directing an art center. It was more than he could handle."

Sam opened the car door. "What do the police think?" he asked Jane. "Do they have any leads?"

Jane shrugged. "They're baffled. I know they've been out to Aiden's house. He lived in a double-wide in the country. But nobody seems to know much about the man. Certainly there's no obvious reason why anyone would kill him."

"You talked to Aiden, Sam. Remember? That time he came out to the antique mall," Cathy said. "Did he say anything that struck you as unusual?"

"Not really," Sam said. "He seemed a likable enough guy. He was into Western stuff. You know, cowboy art. That's what he came looking for."

"Did he shop at the antique mall a lot?" Jane asked.

"Nah, not really. Maybe a couple of times. Back a few years ago. We didn't have what he was looking for. It's the wrong part of the country for cow skulls and Indian bead work." Sam slid out of the back seat. "Listen, I'm already going to be late for my meeting, so I better get going. You never know about Atlanta traffic." He walked around to the driver's side of the car and leaned over to give Cathy a peck on her cheek. "I doubt if I'll get home for supper. I'll call and let you know."

Cathy waited until Sam had started up his car, then she drove out of the lot. "Wow, that's really shocking news about Aiden," she said to Jane. "A murder at our little art center. In Atkinsville, of all places. It's hard to wrap my mind around it."

"I agree. The whole thing strikes me as weird," Jane said. "An old cemetery collapsing into that bomb shelter was weird enough. And then to find Aiden's body in there."

Cathy helped Jane into the house and offered to fix her lunch, but Jane was eager to be alone with her thoughts. After Cathy let herself out, Jane popped two pieces of bread in the toaster to make herself a sandwich, then unscrewed the cap on the bottle of Advil. Her ankle was feeling a little better after sitting in the car, but it was still achy. She removed the orthopedic boot, put her foot on a chair, and applied the ice pack as she ate.

After lunch, Jane hopped into the living room, sat on the couch, and positioned the ottoman so she could elevate her leg. She took her phone out of her pocket. Before rehearsal, she'd put it on Airplane Mode so it wouldn't ring or buzz while they sang. When she lit up the screen, she noticed there was a text from Beau Strickland: Can I come by?

Jane dialed the policeman's number. It went to voice mail, and she left him a message: "I'm home now, if this is a good time for you to come by. I should be here for the rest of the day."

She opened her notebook to her page of questions and laid it beside her so she'd remember what she wanted to discuss with him. Then she picked up the TV remote. Before she pressed the power button, Lotus chirped a feline greeting and hopped onto the ottoman. She padded onto Jane's lap, kneaded for a few seconds, then nuzzled Jane's chin before curling into a humming ball. The cat's purring was so comforting that Jane put down the remote and shut her eyes - just for a minute.

Jane awoke to the sound of the door opening. Lotus leaped off her lap and scurried into the kitchen.

"It's Officer Strickland, Miss Roland. Guess I woke you up?" He shut the door behind him. "You know, you really ought to keep this door locked, ma'am. I'm sure this is a safe neighborhood and all, but as a police officer, I feel obliged to mention it. I tell my mother the same thing. A woman living alone, especially. You just never know."

"You're right," Jane said. "And I usually do. I was just so tired when I got home from choir practice."

"I'm sorry, ma'am," Strickland said. "If this is a bad time, I can...."

"No, please, have a seat. I feel much better, now. The ice pack helps, and I took some Advil with lunch. I've been wanting to talk with you. Oh, and by the way, please call me Jane."

"Yes, ma'am, Jane," Strickland said. When he grinned, Jane noticed that he had a dimple in his right cheek. "And you can call me Beau."

Jane smiled to herself. She expected there were plenty of young women who would be thrilled to call this handsome young fellow 'beau!'

Reaching for her notebook, Jane said, "I've got a couple of things that I wanted to talk with you about. But, first, I forgot to ask you about how Aiden died. Are the police releasing that information?"

"Yes, ma'am. Um, Miss Jane. The cause of death was a blow to the back of the head. There was bruising on the body, too. We think he'd been in a scuffle, and he fell. Maybe hit his head."

"So, you think Aiden got beaten up?" Jane said. "In that old burial vault? I'm surprised the wall didn't cave in during the fight."

Strickland shook his head. "The state crime techs haven't finished going through all the evidence yet. We're not sure if he was killed there or someplace else."

"If he was killed someplace else, then somebody would have had to carry his body into the vault." Jane tried to imagine how somebody could have gotten a body into the burial vault. "You think they dug down into the vault from the grassy area behind AAC?"

"There weren't any signs of digging in that field," Strickland said. "The grass roots go down a pretty good way and form a tight mat. So the killer must have gone through the AAC tunnel and the bomb shelter, then into the vault."

"You're saying that somebody dug a hole through the wall and put Aiden's body into the casket. Then they repaired the hole?"

Strickland nodded. "I can't say for sure, yet. But that's what we're suspicioning."

"And that's why the wall collapsed?" Jane continued. "Because it was weakened by the digging?"

"That'd be my guess."

"So, somebody must have known about the old cemetery," Jane said. "I wonder why they would have kept it secret?" Jane stared at the policeman. "You think maybe they were using the vault to store something illegal? Like drugs? Did you find any drugs?"

"No," Strickland replied. "Nothing obvious. If the vault had been used as a storage area for illegal substances, there could be traces in the dirt floor, so the state crime lab is doing soil analysis. Do you have any reason to suspect that Mr. Parson was using anything? Opioids? Heroin?"

"No, but the women that I paint with say that Aiden smelled of liquor," Jane said.

Strickland nodded.

"And you know he was divorced?" Jane said. "I think his ex had moved out of the area. From some remarks he made, I don't think the divorce was amicable."

"We're trying to locate the ex-wife," Strickland said. "Do you know if she goes by her married name, Parson?"

"No idea. I haven't talked to anybody who actually met her," Jane said. "But I'll keep asking around."

"I appreciate that. And you said there was a brother - in your message. Any idea how to locate him?"

"No," Jane said. "But I could do some checking."

"That'd be real helpful, Miss Jane," Strickland said. "We're a small department, the Atkinsville police. The state crime lab folks are helping us some. But we don't have a lot of investigators. And this is a - I don't know - peculiar case. What with the old cemetery, and all."

Jane smiled. "Okay, I'll see what I can find out. If I discover something, is it okay if I text you?"

"Sure thing." He smiled at her, then stood up. "You feeling well enough to walk me to the door?"

Jane looked at him, a puzzled expression on her face. Would it be rude to tell him that he knew the way out?

"I surely hate to make you get up, Miss Jane," Strickland said, "with your injury and all. But you remember how we talked about you living alone? And the importance of locking your door? Well, if you're going to be offering your help with a police investigation into a murder, it's especially important for you to be careful. You never know who's out there, who's watching."

Jane chuckled. "You don't think anyone's going to come after me," she said. "This is a small town. Everybody knows each other. There aren't any secrets in Atkinsville."

Strickland cocked his head to one side and gestured with his right hand. "Exactly ...."

Jane nodded. "Okay. I see what you mean." She hoisted herself up and hobbled to the front door.

CHAPTER SIXTEEN

Both cats were prowling around the kitchen, yowling for breakfast, when Jane's phone chimed in with its tinny minuet. Clamping the phone between her cheek and shoulder, she said, "Hello."

"You awake?" Pam said.

"You realize that's a question with only one answer."

Pam chuckled. "Never thought about it, but I guess you're right. Astute analysis, Shirley Holmes. Anyway, I'm calling to see if you have rehearsal today."

"Nope, we've got the day off." Jane finished shoveling lumps of smelly wet cat food into two bowls and set them on the tiled floor. Blissful silence pervaded the kitchen as the cats crouched over their bowls.

"Good. How about you button up your London Fog overcoat? I'm itching to go do some sleuthing."

"What do you have in mind, my dear Pamson?" Jane asked.

"Well, I just talked to Betsy, and she said she'd be up for a shopping trip. I figured it would take two of us to keep you safe on your crutches. I did think about taking Tillie, but I don't dare trust her in a store. Especially around anything delicate. Her tail would knock everything off the shelves."

"And what is it that we're shopping for that requires two bodyguards - or a big drooling dog - to keep me safe?"

"She doesn't always drool," Pam protested. "Only when people are eating in front of her." Pam paused. "Well, now that you say it, I guess sometimes she drools even when I'm not eating in front of her. It's the

Newfoundland in her. You know Newfy's are first cousins to Labs? That breed is famous for drooling."

"Um, about the reason for the shopping trip?"

"Oh, yeah. Antiques."

"Ah. Now I understand. You want to go to that antique mall," Jane said. "Where Tony Keller works. I thought that place gave you a bad feeling."

"It did," Pam said. "That's why I invited Betsy to come along. She's the no-nonsense type. Tony Keller wouldn't dare mess with her."

Jane started chuckling. "I'm not sure Betsy would be any match for a criminal in the real underworld. But I suppose I'd trust her to keep us safe in broad daylight in a little country antique mall."

"So, you'll go? Great! I'll come by about 11."

Jane hesitated. Her ankle had gotten achy during the rehearsal yesterday. "I don't know how long I can stand up. But I guess I'll be okay. I could always go sit in your car if my ankle starts throbbing."

"I don't think we'll be there for too long," Pam said. "I thought we could go to Christina's for lunch afterwards, if you're up for it."

Jane said she thought the outing would be good for her. Plus, she was curious about Tony Keller, the man who ran the mall and had run amok at the reception.

At quarter past 11, Pam pulled into the driveway. Betsy helped Jane navigate the walkway with her crutches. "You're doing great with those things," Betsy said with exaggerated enthusiasm. "Some people never get the hang of it, but you're popping along like a pro."

"I bet you say that to all the patients," Jane said.

"I do," Betsy admitted. "It's a good idea to encourage my patients. Especially my older patients."

Jane rolled her eyes. "Thanks."

"Seriously, you're doing a fine job. I'm proud of you." Betsy opened the door to the back, so Jane could plop in. Then Betsy tucked the crutches into the trunk, shut Jane's door, and got into the front passenger's seat. "All set," she announced. "Let's go flush this rat out of his hole."

"Are we actually shopping for anything?" Jane asked as they pulled out of the driveway. "Or is this window shopping with an eye to finding concealed evidence?"

"I'm looking for chandeliers," Pam said.

"Seriously?" Jane said. "As in, more than one?"

Pam nodded enthusiastically. "As many as I can find."

Jane thought about Pam's house, with its sleek, polished wood floors, Japanese paper screens, and hand-thrown ceramics. She couldn't picture a room where Pam could display a chandelier - not where it would blend with the rest of the decor, anyway.

"Are you planning to redecorate?" Jane asked.

"Decorate," Pam said. "Not redecorate."

"You have a room that hasn't been decorated? Like a spare bedroom or something?" Jane took a mental walk through Pam's house. She hadn't ever noticed a bare room. Maybe there was an unfinished room in the attic that she'd never seen?

"Not a room," Pam said. "The pool."

"You're going to hang chandeliers around a pool?" Betsy exhaled loudly, as if punched. "Well, there's an unexpected spot for a touch of elegance!"

Pam started laughing. "Not expensive chandeliers," she said. "Those tinkly ones. With all the sparkly teardrops. I want to hang them on the trellis. And string them along the wire that holds the outdoor lights. It'll make a nice rainbow effect when the sun shines on the glass. Or, at night, when the outdoor lights are on."

"I see," Betsy said, nodding. Jane watched Betsy's facial expression and decided that she didn't see, at all. She was humoring Pam.

"I'm glad we have something to shop for. Maybe even buy," Jane said. "That ought to make Tony Keller friendlier. It won't seem like we've come to spy on him. Even if we really have come to spy on him."

Pam parked as close to the building as she could, so Jane wouldn't have far to maneuver with her crutches. When they entered the long building, they saw several shoppers milling around. A young couple dressed in jeans and tees was squatting down, checking the price tags on tables and desks.

They looked like university students. A heavyset woman carrying a large, square pocketbook was thumbing through a stack of linens. The mall was bursting with knick-knacks - old books, porcelain dolls, and furniture with carved legs. It smelled like a combination of furniture polish and musty porch pillows.

At the cash register, Tony Keller was chatting with an older couple. He looked up when Pam, Betsy, and Jane came in. Jane watched him hoist one hip onto the counter as he listened to the couple. He was wearing a navy blue Henley shirt tucked into belted khaki slacks. Although he had a chunky nose and a stocky build, he looked neat and presentable. Nothing about him - not his clean-shaven face, not his leather loafers, not his short brown hair - looked ominous or threatening. As the three of them began to wander through the shelves, Tony called out, "If you're looking for anything in particular, let me know. There's a lot to see. It can be overwhelming."

"Thank you, I will," Pam answered.

Betsy whispered, "Well, he seems nice enough. Even a rat is a model citizen in his own hole."

They strolled toward the back end of the building, where light fixtures were hanging from ceiling hooks. Pam made a beeline toward an oversized round chandelier with multiple rows of long, slim glass beads. It must have measured 3 feet across and almost that in length, Jane thought. Probably, it once hung above a table in a pretentious dining room. Pam reached up to finger one of the blade-like dangles. Then she turned the price tag over so she could read it.

"That looks awfully heavy," Betsy said. Ever the safety-conscious occupational therapist, she noted, "Sharp, too. If it fell on someone in the pool, it could really injure them."

"Those beads look like skinny daggers," Jane said. She gave an evil grin. "As a matter of fact, if I was going to write a mystery, this would be the perfect chandelier to fall on the murder victim."

"Hmm, I wonder if Tony has noticed that?" Betsy said, grinning back. "Maybe we should buy it quick? Remove it from temptation, as it were. If he ever gets angry again, he could do a lot more damage flinging this thing around than he did with that wine bottle."

"Shh. Keep your voice down. Last thing we want to do is set him off." Jane peeked at Tony, who was still leaning against the counter by the cash register. She didn't think he'd heard them.

Meanwhile, Pam had slid one of the chandelier's dangling blades out of its holder. "I really do like this," she said as she held up the bead to let the light play through it. "It's so over-the-top. I bet it would make intriguing reflections in the water. I wonder if he'd take less for it? It's marked $150. Maybe it's worth that much, but I don't care about it as a light fixture. All I want to do is cannibalize it for these dangles."

As if on cue, Tony hurried up the aisle to join them. "Nice, huh? It's from the '70s, but the style is classic. It'll go with almost any dining room set."

"I'm actually looking for something for my pool," Pam said.

Tony raised his eyebrows. "Oh. And you want a chandelier? Most folks hang a string of lights around a pool. Frosted glass globes or red plastic peppers - that sort of thing." He looked at Pam. "Not that I'm saying a chandelier couldn't work. It'd be a bit, er, unconventional, that's all."

Rather than wasting any more time on the niceties of pool decor, Jane decided to dive right into the subject that had compelled their outing. "Pam's house is a bit unusual. Eccentric, some people might call it. She's an artist, you know, a painter. And a poet. Lots of people from the local art center go to her pool parties. You know about the art center, don't you? AAC?"

Jane watched carefully for any sign that Tony recognized the three of them. All of them had, after all, been in the small hallway at the reception when he'd stormed in and flung the wine bottle. Would he start yelling at them? Kick them out of the antique mall?

"Yeah, I know that place," Tony said. Although he was looking directly at their faces, he didn't seem to remember them. Instead, he leaned closer and spoke in a conspiratorial voice. "I do a bit of painting, myself. Even had a painting in one of their shows." His face turned sour, like he'd swallowed vomit. "I'd be careful there, if I were you. They stole one of my paintings, you know. Gave me one cock-and-bull story after another when I tried to get it back. Doubt if I'll ever see it again. It was pretty nice, too - if I do say so, myself. Not to mention, a real fancy frame on it."

He tilted his head as he faced Pam. "I'll tell you the truth, I wouldn't trust any of them art people. Bunch of phonies. If they come to one of your pool parties, you better count your towels after they leave."

"I'll keep that in mind," Pam said. "Appreciate the advice." She pointed at the chandelier. "How much would you take for this? I don't care about whether it works as a light fixture. I'm not even sure if I'll use the whole thing. But I adore these glass beads. I might just take them off and attach them to the string of lights around my pool. Don't you think they'd make fabulous reflections?"

"What's the tag say?" Tony asked. He reached up to turn it, so he could read the figure. "Hundred and fifty? Well, I can take 10 percent off. That'd make it $135." He looked around, then leaned in, again. "Don't tell Sam - he's the owner - that I said so, but I'll let it go for $125. Aw, call it $120. Now that's a good deal."

"Hmm, I can't pay that much," Pam said. "This is a pool decoration. It's for fun. Not a serious decorator accessory or anything like that."

"Well, how much were you thinking?" Tony asked. He cupped a stubby hand around his chin.

"I don't know. Forty, fifty bucks? Sixty, at the most."

"Sam's the owner of this place?" Jane jumped in. "Sam Barron?" She already knew the answer, but she wanted to steer Tony into talking about the art center, again. "I know his wife Cathy. We sing in choir together."

Tony nodded.

"She's a volunteer at AAC, you know," Jane continued. "In the Angelas. That's the group that fundraises for the art center. Sam sometimes helps her with some of the receptions. For show openings." She tried to emphasize the word, 'receptions,' and reiterated by saying, 'show openings.'

Tony didn't react. Instead, he looked at Pam and said, "I tell you what, this thing's been hanging around here for awhile. Collecting dust. I'll sell it for a hundred. But that's as low as I can go. It's a third off the ticketed price."

"I'll think about it," Pam said. She handed Tony the bead-dagger that she'd removed from the chandelier.

"Ninety-five, and that's my final offer," he answered. "Only one I've got, like this. Might not be here later - after you decide to come back for it."

"I'm willing to take that chance," Pam said.

Jane cocked her head in Pam's direction and looked at Tony. "She drives a hard bargain, doesn't she? It's the starving artist in her. Most artists never have much money. I bet Aiden Parson was always pushing for bargains when he came out here looking for Western memorabilia." She watched Tony's face to see if he'd react to the name. And he did.

"Parson!" he exclaimed. He poked his pudgy forefinger in the air. "That's the name I was trying to remember. The guy who kept putting me off. I wouldn't trust that guy as far as I could throw him."

"He's dead," Jane said.

"Dead? Huh? We talking about the same guy? Long, horsey face? One of those Wyatt Earp mustaches?"

Jane nodded. "That's him. He was the director of the art center."

"Dead. Well, I'll be." Tony seemed genuinely amazed. "That's something. Guess that's why he never answers my calls." He cupped his hand over his mouth and squinted. "Wonder if Sam knows."

"Were they friends?" Jane asked. "Aiden and Sam?"

"I don't know if I'd call them friends," Tony said. "But Parson was out here a lot. Always looking at frames." Tony shrugged. "I guess he liked using old frames for his paintings."

"I didn't know Aiden Parson painted," Betsy said.

Pam had reached up and was gently spinning the chandelier. "None of the beads are damaged. How about seventy? I've got cash," she offered.

Tony kept rubbing his hand over his mouth. "Sure, he painted. You said yourself the man was head of the art center."

Pam began to rifle through her pocketbook. She fished a crumpled bill and some coins out of the bottom. "Look, I've got seventy-five. In cash. That's as high as I can go."

Tony gazed in her direction, but he didn't respond. He was clearly thinking about something other than the sale of the chandelier. He seemed off-balance to Jane, as if the news about Parson had upset him.

"Did you ever see Parson's paintings?" Jane said. "What were they like?"

"Yeah, I saw one. Cowboys and Indians," Tony said. "You know, Indians with those big feather headdresses. Sagebrush, canyons, big sky. It was okay. I'm no expert, that's my opinion is all. I don't think he made any money on it. Folks aren't so much into that sort of thing around here. But that doesn't give him the right to steal somebody else's painting and sell it."

"You think Aiden Parson stole your painting to sell it?" Jane said. "What gives you that idea?"

"The way he looked at it," Tony said. "Staring at it, real close. Like he was studying every one of my brush strokes."

The young university couple had come up behind Tony. The man cleared his throat. "Uh, sir, we're interested in that desk. The one with the rolltop."

Tony turned to follow the man back into the interior of the mall.

Before he walked away, Pam called after him, "Well? Will you take seventy-five?"

Distracted, Tony looked at her. "Yeah, alright." He shook his head, disgusted. "What a bitch!"

Jane looked at Betsy and Pam. Had Tony just called Pam a bitch?

Tony continued muttering as he headed for the cash register. "No way I'll ever get my painting back, now," he said. "It's probably hanging over some rich guy's mantel."

CHAPTER SEVENTEEN

Standing at her doorway, Jane waved as Pam and Betsy drove off. Then - mindful of Officer Strickland's sensible advice - she turned the key and engaged the deadbolt on her door. She hobbled into the kitchen to put the leftover box from Christina's in her fridge and get out her ice pack. Once settled on the living room couch, she removed her surgical boot. Whew! That thing is really uncomfortable, she thought.

The cats peeked into the room. Satisfied their human was alone and the room peaceful, they slipped in. Levi stretched out in front of the heating vent and began giving himself a tongue bath. Lotus jumped on the arm of the couch and chirruped until Jane rubbed her ears. When she'd had enough, Lotus settled onto Jane's lap. Her purring was like a massage. Jane shut her eyes and started replaying the outing in her head.

Pam had been so fixated on that tacky chandelier! The thought made Jane smile now, but she'd gotten exasperated when they were in the antique mall talking with Tony Keller. It seemed like Pam had forgotten the real reason for their trip, which was, after all, not chandelier-hunting but reconnaissance. When Pam had finally made a deal on the thing, they couldn't figure out how they were going to get it home. It was so heavy and awkward. In the end, Tony had found a big cardboard box, padded the bottom with a musty pillow, and laid the chandelier on top. Then he'd carried it out and slid it into the trunk of Pam's car.

During lunch, Pam prattled on and on about her 'find,' while Jane made valiant attempts to reorient the conversation. Jane wanted her friends to help her analyze how Tony had reacted to the news about Aiden's death. Was he genuinely surprised? Or was he covering up? Betsy was of the opinion that the man wasn't bright enough to put on a convincing act. In her opinion, Tony had been genuinely surprised. Pam disagreed. Somehow her analysis brought the discussion back to her prize.

"He was pretty darned foxy about my chandelier. Remember how it was originally marked $150? I'm sure he didn't expect to get anything near that, since he let me bargain him down to $75, just like that." Pam snapped her fingers. "And he put on that show about having to keep the price a secret from his boss. I don't believe a word of it. I bet he made a tidy profit: Fifty bucks - if not more - out of the seventy-five. I think the man's smart. And devious. Definitely capable of murder."

Betsy shook her head. "Remember that big outburst he made at the AAC reception? Everybody heard him shouting. Why would he do that if he was covering up a murder?" Betsy looked at Pam. "It wouldn't make sense, would it? If Tony killed Aiden, he'd want to keep his disagreement with the man a secret. Anybody would be smart enough to figure that out."

Jane wasn't sure what to think. She doubted that Tony was a cold, calculating killer. He and Aiden might have argued about something, and, in the heat of an argument, anything could happen. Tony was built like a bull - strong, heavy. He probably packed a powerful punch. But Betsy had a point - if the man had killed Aiden, why would he call attention to himself at the OCAF reception? Jane wasn't convinced that Tony was a clever person, either - not based on his negotiation over Pam's chandelier, anyway. But was he dumb enough to kill Aiden and then shout about his disagreement with the man?

Although the verdict was still out about Tony Keller, Jane didn't consider the outing a waste of time. They'd learned a couple of things. And - Jane told herself - it was the accumulation of small details which eventually uncovered the truth in a murder investigation. At least, that was true in all the mystery novels that she'd read. And she'd read plenty of them.

The most important new information, Jane thought, was about Aiden. He was a painter - he painted Old West art. Jane thought about this. It went along with Aiden's taste in clothing and his handlebar mustache. It also made sense, since he'd gone to college in Colorado, and he'd worked at a museum that specialized in Western art in Texas. Plus, Win had bumped into Aiden at local venues with live country and western music.

But why didn't Aiden display any of his paintings in his office at AAC? All the previous directors had hung their own work on their walls. Ruth Alice had her colorful collages covering her office walls and her swirling batik scarves draped over her window frames. A director's office was like a personal gallery. It made the director seem in tune with the artists at the center - part of the creative gang, so to speak. Lots of people entered the director's office, and any one of them might be a potential buyer. Displaying your own artwork made sense, from both a public relations as well as a financial point of view. So, why did Aiden choose to keep his artwork a secret?

Maybe he wasn't a particularly talented painter, Jane mused, and he was embarrassed about displaying his paintings? Maybe he'd decided to pursue a career in art administration because he knew he didn't have a future as a painter? Well, his paintings may have been subpar, she thought, but he certainly hadn't displayed any talent as an art administrator. Not at AAC, at any rate.

She wondered whether Aiden had been more successful in his earlier position - at the museum that specialized in Western art in Texas. If that museum had given him a recommendation, they must have been reasonably pleased with his performance. Or maybe not. Jane had heard of companies giving an employee a good recommendation in order to get rid of them. It was definitely unethical, but expedient. If a place wanted to get rid of an employee, then one way to do it was to help the employee secure a job elsewhere.

Jane sat up and reached for her laptop. The sudden movement disturbed Lotus, who sprang off her lap. Was it Jane's imagination, or did the cat manage to cast an offended look as she padded over to join Levi at the heating vent?

Opening her browser, Jane Googled 'Aiden Parson.' She was hoping that - like many artists - he had his own website, where he displayed his own paintings and prints. No such luck. There were several websites related to 'Parson,' but they were all churches. Jane frowned.

Perhaps Aiden had been part of an online artists collective or gallery. She paired his name with 'painter,' and a got long list of house painters named Parson. Jane tried typing 'artist,' instead, but all she got was an art supply store called Partson in Indiana. She tried using just the first name, 'Aiden,' but that yielded pages of articles about an actor.

Frustrated, Jane considered other possibilities. Maybe Aiden used a different name for his paintings? Some painters used an art alias, just as some writers use a pen name. She typed in his initials, 'AP,' but she got websites for the AP wire service and the A & P grocery chain. What kind of alias would an artist choose, she wondered? Some people use pet names as their passwords, so perhaps artists chose pet names as their aliases. If she knew his dog's name, she could try that. Maybe she should text Beau Strickland to see if he knew the name of Aiden's dog?

Perhaps the problem with her search was the term 'art.' It was too general. Jane typed Aiden's name and 'Western Art,' and the website for several museums popped up. One was in Gulch, Texas. That must be the museum that Maisie had mentioned; the museum where Aiden had worked before coming to AAC. Jane scrolled down the list and noticed a newspaper article about a gala hosted by the Gulch Museum. She clicked on it, and, there, front and center, was Aiden's photo - handlebar mustache and long, narrow face. He was holding a stemmed glass and standing beside a woman in a low-cut dress, as well as several well-fed men, in what seemed to be a spacious gallery. All the men wore conventional suits and ties - all except Aiden, who was wearing his characteristic cowboy clothing. He'd apparently made a small concession to the formality of the event by donning a bolo tie with a large, irregularly-shaped stone. The picture was black and white, but Jane assumed the bolo's gemstone was turquoise. At least he didn't get any more dressed-up at the Gulch Museum's events than he did at AAC receptions, Jane thought.

She read the caption. The woman was identified as Amblin Parson. Was she Aiden's wife? Or a relative? Jane scrutinized the photo. The woman didn't look old enough to be his mother or young enough to be his daughter, but she could have been a sister or wife. Although she wasn't what you might call beautiful, there was nothing unattractive about her. She had long, dark hair, which fell loosely to her shoulders and dipped into the cleavage of her skimpy bodice, and she was wearing a bandanna tied around her neck. Jane compared the faces of Amblin and Aiden, feature to feature. If there was any family resemblance other than dark hair, it wasn't obvious.

Jane quickly read through the rest of the article, but it was a puff piece and didn't offer much information. How could she find out if Amblin was married to Aiden? Amblin was an unusual first name. She Googled 'Amblin Parson' and got a screen asking her to clarify: "Did you mean Ramblin Amblin?" Jane clicked yes, and a website popped up, titled, 'Ramblin Out West with Amblin.' Sure enough, it was an artist's website, and it featured a large photo of Amblin wearing a 10-gallon hat, paintbrush in hand, standing in Western surroundings. Her cowboy-style shirt was skin tight, and the snaps were unsnapped far enough down her chest to make it clear that she hadn't snapped on a bra. There was an easel behind her, and it displayed a painting in splashy colors of a muscled woman riding bareback - and bare-breasted - out of a blurry backdrop. The subject's nipples were the same garish red as a bandanna that flapped in the breeze.

Jane went to the 'Gallery' section and clicked through pages of paintings by Amblin and "Honey Pie." All of Amblin's paintings featured vivid, bold swaths of color and larger-than-life subjects in Western states and various states of undress. There were fewer paintings by Honey Pie, and they were much more subdued and traditional, picturing cowboys and cattle, cacti and colts. Jane wondered if Honey Pie was Aiden. She enlarged several of those paintings but couldn't tell if there was a signature.

If Amblin was, indeed, Aiden's ex, where was she now? Jane clicked the 'Contact' button and brought up a box for sending an email to Amblin's agent, Enid Ruskind. Jane typed out a message: "Trying to reach Amblin, wife of Aiden Parson." She hesitated. Maybe Amblin was Aiden's sister? Or cousin? Jane frowned. Even if Amblin was only a cousin, she should still be notified about the death. But how much should Jane reveal in her email? She typed: "Have important news about Aiden," and her phone number.

Before pressing 'Send,' Jane sat, staring at the message. Would it be overstepping to send it? After all, it was the police's job to notify next of kin - wasn't it? And, what would she say when Amblin called her? If there was any chance that Amblin - whether wife or relative - had been involved in Aiden's murder, Jane didn't want to sabotage the investigation by revealing too much.

Jane picked up her phone and scrolled to Officer Strickland's contact. When Beau picked up, she explained that she'd located a painter named Amblin Parson, who might have been Aiden's wife.

"Yup, that's her," Strickland said. "Found her in public records."

"Were they still married?" Jane said. "I didn't see any mention of Aiden on her website. Or where she lives."

"She's got a condo in Chicago," Strickland said.

"So, you talked with her? And informed her about Aiden's death?"

"Yup."

"And did she seem upset?" Jane asked. "I imagine it must be pretty shocking - to learn that your husband, or your ex-husband, was found murdered."

"Hard to tell much about a person's reaction on the phone," Strickland said. "Mrs. Parson said they never bothered to get a divorce. But it seems they haven't lived together in a few years."

"I wonder why they didn't get a divorce," Jane said.

"Mrs. Parson says there was no point, since Aiden would never make enough money to pay her alimony."

"Whoa!" Jane said. "Doesn't sound like that was the happiest of marriages. I guess she'll be happy to get the money from selling the house. Assuming they owned it."

"They did, but she didn't seem to care about it," Strickland said. He chuckled. "Matter of fact, she called it Aiden's 'redneck shack.' I told her the place was likely hers, unless there was some other provision in a will. She said Aiden was too scatter-brained to make a will. Then she told me to get rid of the place, however we wanted. And we should send the money to his brother. Because she was sick and tired of the people at the care home pestering her about money. She said she'd figured out how to make an honest living on her own, now Aiden was out of her life, and she didn't see how her husband's brother was her problem, anymore."

"Doesn't sound like she's got any lingering affection for her man. But I guess she's doing okay for herself as an artist, now," Jane said. "Have you been on her website - by any chance - and seen her paintings?"

Jane wasn't sure, but she thought she heard Strickland giggling as he answered. "Yes, ma'am, I have. Closeups of the Wild West." He emphasized the word, 'wild.'

"Actually, I'd be tempted to call them pinups of the Wild West," Jane said. She couldn't help grinning as she pictured Strickland rambling through Amblin's Gallery. "Did you see that there was another painter featured in her gallery, too? She called him Honey Pie. Way different style than Ramblin Amblin. Do you think that could be Aiden's work? Aiden was a painter, too, you know. Did Old West art."

"I'm not one to judge, but Honey Pie's paintings look more like my idea of Western art."

"Mine, too," Jane said. "I wasn't sure if they were signed. I tried to enlarge a few of the paintings, but either the resolution wasn't good enough, or my computer's not good enough."

"I'll take another look," Strickland said. "We have a pretty good computer here. And one of the officers, he's a whiz at this technical stuff."

"Well, call me if you need help tracking the art," Jane said. "It would be interesting to know if Aiden pulled in much money from his painting. I'm not a specialist in Western art, but I probably have more time to investigate than you do."

"Will do," Strickland said. "I'll go get John and take another look, right now."

As soon as she said goodbye, she texted the painters in her Tuesday watercolor group:

Check out this website: 'Ramblin Out West with Amblin ' AMBLIN IS AIDEN'S WIFE!!!!!

Then she settled back - a grin as wide as the Texas sky spread across her face - to await the inevitable reactions. If only she'd been a fly on the wall to watch dimple-faced Beau Strickland studying the art of Ramblin Amblin and Honey Pie!

CHAPTER EIGHTEEN

Jane checked her phone messages as soon as she woke up. She saw a dot by the Tuesday watercolor group and figured there would be a chain of funny comments about Ramblin Amblin. But she resisted the urge to read them. She had to get moving if she was going to get herself ready for a 9 o'clock rehearsal.

At quarter to 8, Cathy Barron called and offered to come by and pick her up. "Thanks, Cathy, but I really need to get used to driving myself," Jane explained. "I don't like depending on anyone else. Makes me feel helpless."

"Well, if you run into problems, call me," Cathy said. "I can come over and get you. Even at the last minute. It's not any bother at all."

"That's awfully sweet of you," Jane said. "But I think I'll be fine. I've been working out a plan for how to get my crutches into the car. And I just switched my wallet and stuff from a pocketbook to a small backpack. That way, I'll have my arms and hands free."

Before they hung up, Jane said, "By the way, I've been trying to learn more about Aiden Parson. The more I think on it, the more I realize that I didn't know him very well. My own fault. I didn't like the job the man was doing, so I just assumed I didn't like him. Anyway, turns out he was a painter. Western-style art. His wife was, too. Did you know that?"

"No, I had no idea," Cathy said. "Never met his wife. I don't remember seeing Aiden's paintings at any of the AAC shows. I guess maybe it would have been a conflict of interest for him to enter them, since he was the organization's director. All Sam ever said was that Aiden liked old frames.

You know, the fancy gold ones, with swirly edges. I never thought about what Aiden did with the frames. But it makes sense he'd want them for his paintings."

"Yes, that makes sense," Jane said. "Maybe ask Sam what he knew about Aiden's paintings? No rush - next time you think about it. The more we learn about Aiden, the better the chance the police can figure out who killed him."

"Well, now, everybody says you are quite the Murder She Wrote! Sounds like you're on this case." Cathy chuckled. "But, seriously, Jane, you're not thinking anyone around here killed him? Atkinsville is such a close-knit little community. Why would anybody want to kill the director of a teensy art center?"

"It is hard to imagine," Jane said. "But somebody did it. Aiden's body was in that cemetery. It had to get there somehow. I can't imagine that a random killer would have known about that place. I mean, I've been active at AAC for years, and I never knew there was a cemetery backed up to the old bomb shelter."

"Ooh, that place has always given me the creeps," Cathy said. "Just the thought of the tunnel - let alone that nasty little room - makes me shudder."

After returning from rehearsal, Jane settled herself on the couch. She was feeling pretty confident about her ability to get around. The trip to choir rehearsal had also been a rehearsal of her independence in spite of the crutches. As she propped her leg on the ottoman, Jane removed the orthopedic boot and iced down her ankle. Then she picked up her phone, switched it off Silent Mode, and checked her messages. Sure enough, there was a long chain from the Tuesday watercolor painters. Ramblin Amblin had started a stampede!

Most of the messages had been written last night. Grace had been the first to respond to Jane's text. She wrote:

Good grief!!!

Maisie's comment:

Tee Hee. No false sense of modesty

Grace wrote:

No modesty at all

Ever practical, Betsy wrote:

Bet she sells more paintings than we do

Pam chipped in:

Good thing Amblin was not into plein air painting! She would get arrested for public indecency

Betsy wrote:

If she used models, she would get arrested for abuse. Imagine posing outdoors in those skimpy outfits! Frigid winters out West

Grace wrote:

Frigid? Nothing frigid about her. Is this Western art or body art?

Betsy replied:

Bawdy art

Donna rarely checked her messages. But this morning, she'd apparently noticed the chain and added her two cents to it:

Just showed paintings to Bill

Pam wrote:

Did he like?

Donna wrote:

He wants me to start a Ramblin group at AAC

Pam wrote:

He wants to be your Honey Pie?

Maisie texted to ask if Jane had shown Amblin's site to Ruth Alice, who had a degree in art history.

Good Idea. Will do that now

Jane forwarded the Ramblin Amblin site to Ruth Alice. Then she tried to think of a clever rejoinder to add to her friends' string of comments. Before she managed to come up with anything, a text came through from Beau Strickland:

Did you ever look into Parson's brother? Alden Parson

Oops! Jane had forgotten that she'd said she was going to investigate Aiden's brother. Looking at Beau's text, she assumed the policeman had typed too fast and entered Aiden's first name instead of his brother's. She started to text him to ask the brother's first name, then she squinted at the screen and realized he had typed 'Alden' - off by one letter from Aiden.

She replied:

On it now. Do you know where Alden is?

Beau texted:

No

Jane's notebook was on the couch. She reached for it and opened to a fresh page. On the top, she wrote,

Aiden's Brother - Alden

She remembered Pam said the brother had a medical condition, and he required Aiden's help. On the first line, Jane wrote, "medical condition," followed by a question mark.

Jane skipped down a few lines and wrote the words, "where he lives." Pam had said the brother was in a facility somewhere out West. Amblin had confirmed that he was in a care home when she complained that the place was pestering her for money.

Jane decided her first step should be finding this care home. Perhaps it was in Aiden's hometown? Jane didn't know where Aiden had grown up, but - if their parents were deceased - then Aiden might have moved his brother to a nearby facility, where Aiden could visit him. Jane knew Aiden had been at the University of Colorado. Which campus, she wondered? There were campuses in three big cities - Boulder, Denver, and Colorado Springs. Was it Grace's boyfriend who had known Aiden in Colorado? Hmm. Jane was about to text Grace to ask which campus, but then she decided to start her search with Aiden's last place of employment, instead. That was the museum in Gulch, Texas. Didn't Pam say that Aiden had placed his brother there? It would be a lot easier to find him if he was in a smaller town like Gulch.

She looked up all the facilities for adults with disabilities in the Gulch area. But Jane hesitated before starting to make calls. Would a care home answer questions about their patients? Most medical institutions had strict rules about privacy. Perhaps Jane could say she was calling from the Atkinsville Police Department? Then again, that would get awkward if she had to leave a callback message.

Suddenly, she had a brainstorm: Why not start her probe by calling the Gulch Museum of Western Art? Surely, they wouldn't have as many regulations regarding privacy as a medical facility. Maybe Jane would get lucky and connect with somebody who'd worked with Aiden. Knew about him as a painter. Perhaps knew his wife Amblin or even his brother.

On her first call, Jane struck gold. The woman who answered the phone identified herself as Wynetta Macklin and said she'd been volunteering at the museum ever since Aiden was the director. Wynetta was at the front desk. She seemed to have plenty of time to talk. And was she ever a talker! From the sound of her twang, Jane pictured Wynetta as an older woman with teased hair, a fringed leather jacket, heavy silver hoops in her ears, and leatherette cowboy boots on her feet. In other words, a Texas version of Dolly Parton.

Jane made up a story to explain her call. "Aiden's told me so much about your museum," Jane said. "I just love art, you know, and I'm coming out your way in a couple of months. If I've got enough time, I want to come visit the museum."

"Oh, you should, you'll love it. When you planning to come?" Wynetta asked. Without waiting for an answer, she charged right along. "It gets real blowy here in winter. But, in spring, the weather is simply GORGEOUS. Have you ever been to Texas Hill Country? Green, oh it's so green, here. It's really something." She lowered her voice as if to share a confidence. "You know, we call the Hill Country our state secret. THE biggest secret in THE biggest state."

"No, I've never been there," Jane said. "I've spent a little time in Houston. And I visited Dallas and Fort...."

"Oh, no, Hill Country is nothing like those citified places!" Wynetta gushed. "Ugh, they're so ugly. Flat. Dusty. Sure they have plenty of oil money, but nothing to look at. I'll tell you what, here's where money comes on vacation. Know what I mean? Green attracts green. That's what we say."

"Well, you're definitely making me want to visit," Jane said. "Aiden always said great things about your collection, too."

"It's the best Western art museum in the country. Bar none," Wynetta said. "Like I said, green attracts green. You wouldn't believe the amount of support we get from our members. I mean, we are talking OIL paintings - made of OIL money, Hon."

"Sounds wonderful," Jane said. "I guess Aiden has always been good at attracting donors? And his wife - I think her name is Amblin - she's an artist, too? Or so I hear."

"Yes, we have two of her paintings," Wynetta said in a less than enthusiastic voice. "In the upstairs gallery. That's where we keep our contemporary collection. Not my favorite, but everybody has their own taste in art. Including the oil barons - read "menfolk" - who donate the money for acquiring new paintings. You haven't seen any of her work, I guess? She does big canvasses. Bright, splashy colors. And her subjects - well, they're, I don't know, off-key, I guess you might say. Controversial."

"Really," Jane said, "but Aiden's work isn't like that, is it?"

"Oh, no, not at all. He does what I'd call classical Western art. Full of detail. Like you could reach out and touch the cowboy's face. Feel his leathery skin, the sun on his neck. You could swear the feathers were plucked from a real bird. Every single tuft." Wynetta paused, and Jane could hear her welcoming somebody. Then she came back on the line. Her voice had turned into a purr. "Would you mind if I put you on hold, Hon? Or you could call back. I've got somebody at the desk. Real nice couple. I'm gonna stamp their tickets and give them a teensy little finger walk through this brochure that has a map of each floor."

"No problem, I'll be glad to wait," Jane said. Since Wynetta seemed to be such an overflowing cornucopia of information, Jane didn't want to risk losing their connection. Wynetta's voice switched off, and prerecorded music began to play. Jane sat through a full rendition of Gene Autry's "Back in the Saddle Again" and most of Marty Robbins' "El Paso," before Wynetta came back on the line.

"You still there?" Wynetta said.

"Yes."

"Oh, I'm so glad I didn't lose you, Hon," Wynetta said. "Lotsa folks are just too impatient, you know? There's no need to be in such a great big hurry. Slow down and smell the sagebrush, that's what I always say. Only got you one life to live, so you may as well enjoy it. So, where were we, now? You're coming to Hill Country? In April, did you say?"

"Not sure exactly when yet," Jane said. "But we were talking about Aiden's paintings. Do you have any of his work on display?"

"Oh, yes, the museum has one of his. A big one. It's in the lobby, just as you come in the building," Wynetta said. "You can't miss it. It's basically a mural - covers the whole wall. Matter of fact, it's on the museum's website. Home page. Right up at the top."

"I'll have a look," Jane said. "And didn't I hear something about how Aiden had a brother, there? It was a sad story, if I remember. Something about a disability?"

Wynetta adjusted her voice down several notches as she answered. "Yes, it's the saddest thing, Hon. The brother - Alden's his name - lives in a nursing home. Right outside Gulch. The Langdon House, I think it's called. You know, Aiden's always been so good to him. You can really read a man's heart by how he treats family. Especially when there's a problem. That's the real true EKG."

"Do you know what's wrong with the brother?" Jane asked.

"One of those rare things," Wynetta said. "Some name like Bell's Palsy. Oh, no, that's not it. Bell's Sickness, maybe. Or Fragile Marker Something. I forget. Anyway, it's one of those gene things. Affects boy children. Makes a person slow in the head. You can tell who's got it by looking at them. Long face, big ears, square jaw. Aiden kinda looks like that, too, so I think maybe he got a touch of it in his genes, too. Not the mental part, though. His brother, he can't talk right. And he kind of walks like a chicken - flaps his hands, stands on his tiptoes. Aiden brought him to a few events at the museum. You know, to get him out for a breather. But he had to stop because his brother got real nervous in strange places. Trembled. Even had a seizure, once."

"That sounds terrible," Jane said. "But it seems like Aiden really looked after his brother, cared about him. Was Amblin good to him, too? You know, motherly?"

"Motherly? Amblin? If she was a mother hen, she'd be the one who pecked her baby chicks to death," Wynetta said. "I never understood what

Aiden saw in that woman. I mean, she made sure you could see plenty of her. The way she dressed didn't leave much to the imagination. Same thing with her paintings."

Suddenly, Wynetta amped up her voice as if she was addressing somebody in the room. "Well, look at you!" Jane heard her exclaim. "It's been a month of Sundays. I swan...." Then Wynetta came back on the line and said, "I'm so sorry, Hon, but I gotta run. Somebody here I need to talk to. Did we get all your questions answered? If not...."

"Yes, you did," Jane said. "You've been very generous with your time, Wynetta, and I appreciate all your help."

"Well, good," Wynetta said. "Hope to see you in Hill Country."

As soon as Jane disconnected, she wrote down Langdon House in her notebook. On the internet, she found a small, privately-run care home by that name about 10 miles outside Gulch. She wrote down the address and phone number, so she could pass it on to Beau.

Then she looked up genetic diseases with names that resembled Bell's and Fragile Marker. Again, Wynetta's information was helpful, if not quite accurate. Martin Bell Syndrome, also called Fragile X Syndrome, was a rare inherited disorder usually found in males. It was caused by a gene mutation and produced severe cognitive impairment, speech difficulty, and hyperactive behavior, as well as motor problems like hand flapping, toe walking, tremors, and seizures. Some people carried the disorder, and they displayed some of the characteristics, but to a lesser degree. In these "premutation carriers," as they were called, mental function was normal. But the disease might cause emotional problems, learning disabilities, even balance and memory problems. For these carriers, symptoms often became more troubling after the age of 50.

Just as Wynetta said, people with Fragile X syndrome displayed a distinct physical appearance - long and narrow face, large ears, prominent jaw and forehead, flat feet, and unusually flexible fingers. Carriers - who had inherited a lesser degree of the disorder - usually shared this same "look." Jane reflected on Aiden's appearance. The description fit him perfectly. She remembered his face, which she'd always thought of as horsey - long and narrow, with a bulging jaw. He had big ears, too. Suddenly, Jane understood why Aiden cultivated that ridiculous handlebar mustache: It distracted from the Fragile X Syndrome features. Thinking back, Jane realized that, yes, Aiden had several of the physical characteristics and not just his face. He definitely had gangly fingers. And he had a gait that could have been caused by flat feet. If a tremor was likely to show up after the age of 50, that could have explained why Aiden might have stopped painting.

Wow! Jane thought about all the implications of this discovery. Aiden must have been under intense financial pressures to support his brother. Plus, Aiden must have known that, as he aged, he was likely to face increasing difficulties with his own motor control. On the Web MD site, Jane read that some of the premutation carriers began to experience memory problems as they aged. Maybe some of Aiden's incompetent administration at AAC was the result of this disorder? To make matters worse, Aiden had married a woman who lacked sympathy. Evidently, she hadn't shown any inclination to help with Alden.

No wonder Aiden Parson had resorted to liquor. The uncertainty of his future must have dominated his thoughts. Jane remembered the many conversations she'd had with AAC members complaining about Aiden's work. She wished she'd known about the difficulties - the terror - that Aiden must have faced every day when he looked at his own face in the mirror.

Her phone began to play its minuet, and Jane snapped back to the present. Ruth Alice's face was on the screen as Jane picked up the phone.

"You got my text?" Jane said. "About Ramblin with Amblin."

"I did. It was very, um, revealing."

"Let me guess what you're going to say." Jane giggled. "It was a bit alarming."

"A bit? Hah! More like a five-alarm fire," Ruth Alice said.

"Wait 'til you hear the rest," Jane said.

CHAPTER NINETEEN

Standing in front of the full-length mirror in her bedroom, Jane inspected her black dress - the dress she'd bought last year to perform at AAC's holiday gala. Thank goodness, it still fit. The last thing Jane wanted to do, while wearing an orthopedic boot and hobbling on crutches, was go shopping for a new dress.

Lotus watched from the foot of the bed as Jane pivoted three-quarters around to make the full skirt swirl. Jane felt the same delight as she did when she was a little girl with a fancy, flouncy skirt. Sunlight twinkled on the sequins decorating the fitted bodice and sleeves. From the minute she'd seen it, Jane had fallen in love with this dress - it was simple and elegant, with just enough eclat. Perfect for a choir member who wanted to blend in with her fellow singers but also wanted to sparkle on stage.

Jane's eyes slid down to the orthopedic boot, which peeked out from below the ankle-length hem. The boot was barely noticeable, she thought. After all, the audience would be focusing on the singers' faces, not their shoes. But, now that she was considering her feet, what should she wear on her other foot? Jane reached for a shoebox on the top shelf in her closet. She opened the box and was greeted with a whiff of leather. Jane took out a black pump and slipped it on her right foot. She tried walking, pump on one foot and orthopedic boot on her left leg. This will probably be alright, Jane thought. The pump was fairly comfortable, and she felt stable on it.

After replacing the dress on its velvet hanger and enclosing it in the plastic dry-cleaner's bag, Jane dressed in pants and a tunic-sweater. She hobbled down the stairs with Lotus following patiently. After a few steps, the cat darted around her and scampered down the rest of the stairs. Jane glanced at the clock on the living room mantle. Ruth Alice should be arriving any minute. She'd called first thing this morning and announced she was bringing a lesson on Western art, to give Jane a general understanding of Aiden's and Amblin's art. The lesson was going to encompass an edible component, as well, so Ruth Alice had told Jane to save her appetite for a "rodeo" brunch.

Rodeo brunch was a Western omelette that Ruth Alice had gotten from the little deli near Christina's. It was tasty, and Ruth Alice had brewed sage tea to go with it. But the dessert was the most memorable part of the meal: A honey pie!

"It's an old family recipe," Ruth Alice explained. "Really, it's just custard pie, but honey is the main sweetener. So my family always called it 'honey pie.'"

"You're kidding!" Jane said. "How perfect is this? Mmm," she said, as she lifted the dishcloth covering the pie. "It smells glorious."

"Wait 'til you taste it," Ruth Alice said. "I promise it'll knock your cowboy boots off." She took a sip of the tea.

"Hmm. Do you think it'll work on an orthopedic boot?"

Ruth Alice expelled a mouthful of tea with her laugh. "Well, I dunno, pardner. But I guess we're fixin' to find out."

After eating, Ruth Alice began her lesson. "Western art is about subject matter, rather than style," she explained. "It presents a romanticized view of the lives of cowboys and indigenous people."

Jane leafed through the coffee table book of Western art that Ruth Alice had brought along. "Looks like posters for John Wayne movies," Jane said.

"Whoa!" Ruth Alice hollered. "Aren't you quick on the draw! These artists did influence Hollywood, especially Charles Russell. The paintings were like ads for an imaginary American West. Idyllic landscapes. A sense of adventure. The paintings actually encouraged people to go settle in the West."

"Was this art taken seriously?" Jane asked. "I could see how some art critics might have considered the paintings hokey. You know, commercial tripe."

Ruth Alice nodded. "That's exactly how Frontier Art was viewed at first, when painters started doing it around the 1840s. Critics said the paintings were contrived. Propaganda art. But, over the decades, it's gotten its share of admirers. Now there's a Cowboy Artists of America Society. And some of the artists are highly respected. I'm sure you've heard of George Caitlin. And the vistas painted by Bierstadt. The two most famous painters were Russell and Remington." Ruth Alice thumbed to a chapter on Frederic Remington and flipped through the pages to show Jane the reproductions.

"Hey, hold your horses, Cowgirl," Jane said. She opened her laptop and clicked on the Gulch Museum's home page. At the top was Aiden's hallway mural. "Aiden's mural looks like a dead ringer for these Remington paintings. Doesn't it?"

"It really does," Ruth Alice agreed. "He must have studied Remington's technique."

Jane glanced at the clock on her laptop. "Ooh, I've got to get going, Ruth Alice. I think I told you that our Tuesday watercolor group is meeting at Pam's this afternoon? I hate to eat and run. Er, eat and hobble. But we're starting at one, and I'm already late."

Although the Tuesday watercolor group usually gathered in the AAC kitchen to paint, they couldn't meet there today. During the weeks leading up to the gala, the kitchen was transformed into a multi-purpose collection area for the event: holiday decorations, items in the silent auction, and serving ware for the banquet.

Ruth Alice picked up their brunch dishes and stacked them in the dishwasher. "I'm leaving you the rest of the honey pie," she told Jane.

Jane started to object.

"I made two of them - and, as much as I love it, a whole pie is more than enough for me. So I'm donating all the calories from this one toward the healing and recuperation of Jane Roland's ankle."

"Thanks," Jane said. "But I just tried on my dress for the gala. To make sure it still fits."

Ruth Alice raised her eyebrows as she waited for Jane's report on the dress.

"I'm happy to report that I don't need to shop for a new dress," Jane said. "But I can't be sure that honey pie is going to squeeze into that bodice with me. If you don't mind, I think I'll take it to Pam's and introduce the other painters to edible Western art."

"Sounds like a roundup to me."

"Can I borrow your book?" Jane asked. "I want to show them Aiden's mural alongside Remington's paintings."

During the short drive to Pam's house, Jane kept thinking about Aiden's mural. She was impressed by his skill, as well as his ability to capture the essence of Remington's style. Jane had never tried to imitate another artist's work. But a lot of artists, especially in earlier centuries, began their art training as apprentices. Hired to work in the master's studio, they mixed pigments and prepared canvasses. Then, they graduated to painting portions of the master's work. Trying to reproduce an artist's style would force a student to examine the master's work closely, as well as absorb unspoken lessons about composition, tone, and brushwork. Jane decided that she'd try teaching herself about Western art by this method, today - she'd imitate one of the paintings in Ruth Alice's book during the painting session at Pam's house.

Fistfights and guns were prominent elements of the imaginary West portrayed by this art and enshrined by Hollywood. Jane thought about Aiden's violent death. It was more than ironic that he'd died from a beating. Murdered. As a devotee of Frontier art, Aiden had, in a sense, died in the style he'd painted.

When she got to Pam's house, Jane parked by the front stairs and texted for help. There was no way she was going to be able to carry in honey pie - not with crutches. And certainly not with Tillie's inevitable greeting.

Maisie and Grace came outside and brought in the pie, the coffee table book, and Jane's painting gear. Betsy helped Jane get out of the car and onto her crutches, then helped Jane hobble along the gravel path and up the stairs to the front door. When Tillie loped over to say hello, Betsy grabbed the dog's collar and ordered her - in a forceful voice - to sit. To Jane's astonishment, the dog did.

"Well, I'm impressed," Jane said. "Did they teach you how to talk to dogs in Occupational Therapy school?"

Betsy grinned. "No, but they taught us how to talk to patients. They're not so different."

Upstairs, the painters had spread out their easels around Pam's large, modern living space, which served as a den, dining area, and parlor. The only demarcations between the areas were Japanese paper screens, and Pam folded or rearranged these to accommodate activities at her home.

Before setting up her easel, Jane plunked herself down on the couch and invited Tillie to come and slobber her greeting. Jane figured it was best to get the dog's initial enthusiasm over with, and do it from the relative safety of Pam's sturdy leather couch.

As Tillie swabbed her ears and chin, Jane called out, "Hey, Pam! Hey, everybody! Tillie smells like wine. Did somebody leave a glass where she could reach it?"

"Ugh. It must be me. My glass is knocked over," Grace said. She stood up. "I'm going to go wash it out and get a refill. Do you want some wine, Jane?"

"Oh, wait," Pam said. "Before y'all settle in, come out here and look at the pool."

Grace, Betsy, Maisie, and Jane followed Pam out the sliding glass doors to the covered porch, which overlooked the backyard pool and surroundings. Wires on tall poles encircled the pool and held small lightbulbs. Pam had strung the chandelier dangles along the wires.

"Wait 'til the sun goes down a little," Pam said, "and I'll turn on the lights. The beads really twinkle. It's Van Gogh's 'Starry Night', and then some."

"Looks lovely," Grace said. "What an unusual touch!"

"I bet the effect is worth every penny of the 75 bucks you paid Tony for that chandelier," Betsy said.

"Speaking of famous paintings," Jane said, "Ruth Alice came over this morning and gave me a lesson on Western art. I brought her book to show y'all. You're not going to believe...."

"Did that pie come from Ruth Alice, too?" Pam interrupted. "Oh, wait, do I hear a scrabbling noise? Where'd you put that pie? Tillie! Tillie, where are you, Girl?"

Grace didn't wait for the dog to respond to Pam's summons. Instead, she dashed into the kitchen. A few seconds later, they heard Grace's voice: "It's safe, thank goodness. Tillie can't reach that far up on the counter. Although you've got to give her credit for trying. She was just about one tongue-length too short."

"Was she was up on her hind legs when you measured?" Pam asked. "Never trust that dog around food." Pam started for the kitchen.

"It's okay. I moved the pie into the fridge," Grace said as she rejoined them on the porch. "She can't get into the fridge, can she?"

"Not sure." Pam shrugged and gave a goofy grin. "Probably not."

Jane remembered earlier painting sessions at Pam's house - overturned easels and plates of snacks gone missing. "How about if we leave Tillie outside while we paint, today?" she suggested.

"Good idea," Pam said. She opened the screen door leading from the porch to the stairs down to the pool. "Outside, Girl," she said.

Tillie, who had followed Grace onto the porch, looked at Pam. Except for her soulful eyes, she didn't move a muscle.

Betsy strode to the door. In her occupational therapist voice, she commanded, "Tillie, out!"

Immediately, Tillie stood erect and lumbered through the door. They watched her galumph down the wooden steps. Betsy shut the door, popped the latch into the hook, and dusted off her hands.

"Impressive!" Pam said. "Do you give voice lessons?"

Inside, they all began to spread out their easels, fill their water bowls, and squeeze pigments onto their palettes. Jane opened Ruth Alice's book on Frontier art to the chapter on Remington and studied the reproductions. One of the paintings, called "Against the Sunset," showed a cowboy on his moving horse illuminated by a golden sky. Jane thought she could reproduce that background color in quinacridone orange and yellow. The muted tones of the shrubby foreground should also work well with watercolor pigments. Jane was eager to see if she could imitate enough of Remington's style to make a pleasing painting - a painting that paid homage to Remington but had enough original elements to stand on its own - the way Aiden had done with the mural in the Gulch museum.

After everyone had settled down to work, she heard the front door opening. "Hi, everybody!" Donna called from the front hall. "We just got back from an appointment, so Bill drove me over." She came upstairs, with Bill's heavier footsteps following her.

Donna's husband was a tall, powerfully-built man. He had creamy white hair, which fell over the tops of his ears, and a wispy Santa Claus beard that stuck out from the corners of his chin. Ever since Donna had quit driving, Bill usually dropped her off at painters' events. He seemed to enjoy coming in to say hello and see what everybody was painting.

Jane's easel was set up beside the couch, so it was the first one that Bill and Donna noticed. "Wow, look at that - Jane's doing a Western," Donna said to Bill. "Looks like you may get your wish for a Ramblin group, after all."

Bill's booming voice might as well have been a loud speaker. "Nah, this ain't no Ramblin Amblin," he announced. "It's not even a cowgirl. And, look, the fella's got all his clothes on."

The rest of the painters - their curiosity piqued - gathered around Jane's easel.

"Sorry to disappoint you," Jane said, giggling. "But I've never been into nudes. If it's any consolation, there's some honey pie in the fridge."

"Honey pie? What do you mean?" Donna said. She marched over to the fridge and pulled out the pie. "They call this honey pie? Really?"

"That's what Ruth Alice calls it," Jane called. "She said it's an old family recipe. It's a custard pie, but the sweetener is mostly honey."

"I'll have a slice, if you're offering," Bill said.

"Everybody else want some?" Donna called from the kitchen. While she sliced the pie and gathered plates and forks, Bill took a seat on the sprawling easy chair against the wall.

"I thought we were going to work awhile longer, before we took a break," Pam said, as she dunked her brush in her water container. "But I'm not going to turn down honey pie."

"That sounds mighty suggestive to me," Bill said. He winked at Donna as she handed him a slice of pie. "No wonder you ladies like these painting sessions so much."

"None for me," Jane said, as Donna offered her a plate. "I had a piece before I came."

As the painters began to settle on the couch and chairs with plates of honey pie on their laps, Betsy said, "What did Ruth Alice say about Western art, Jane?"

"I bet she was a terrific teacher," Grace said, "That was her major in college, wasn't it? Art history? I wondered whether she thought that Aiden was the Honey Pie on Amblin's website?"

Jane reached for the coffee table book and showed the Remington reproduction that was her painting reference. "Ruth Alice said that...." Just then, her phone minuet began to play. Jane glanced at the screen. It was Beau Strickland.

"Whoa - Hold your horses, pardners," Jane announced. "I got me the sheriff on the line!"

CHAPTER TWENTY

While Jane held her phone to her ear to listen to Officer Strickland, the painters chewed quietly on their honey pie. Strickland had a soft, Southern gentleman's voice that didn't blare through the phone and into the room, so - try as they might - the women could only hear Jane's replies. But these were plenty tantalizing.

When Jane exclaimed, "Wow!" into the phone, the women's ears perked up. And when she said, "Well, there's a motive for murder. Art forgery is big bucks," they all leaned closer, straining to hear.

Without making any sound, Maisie mouthed Jane's words, "Art forgery!?" Her eyes were as wide as the Western sky.

"No, she didn't," Jane said into the phone. "But I only spoke to that one volunteer at the desk. If she did know about the scandal, I'm sure she wouldn't have mentioned it to me."

"Scandal!" Betsy mouthed, her eyebrows raised in an arch higher than McDonald's famed golden arches. Betsy looked around the room and mouthed the word, "Scandal!" again.

"You remember what Amblin told you?" Jane said into the phone. "That she'd figured out a way to make an HONEST living on her own. Maybe that's what she meant - that Aiden was making a dishonest living by peddling fake art."

Focused on his slice of pie, Bill had been ignoring both the conversation and the women's reactions. As soon as he put the last forkful into his mouth, he sat up and announced - in his loud speaker of a voice - "You know, this honey pie is real good. Can't say I've ever heard of it before. But maybe we should look up the recipe...."

The room exploded into a chorus of shushing sounds as all the painters turned on Bill.

Perched on the arm of her husband's chair, Donna whispered, "Quiet," and she put her finger to her lips, as if she was talking to a kindergarten class. She whispered the obvious into Bill's ear: "Jane's on the phone."

"Well, I can see that," Bill said. "But whoever she's talking to can't hear me."

"Shh," came the chorus again.

Jane had to block the microphone with her hand so Beau wouldn't hear her giggling. With so many women shushing Bill, Pam's living room sounded like a snake pit.

Bill looked around the room, a baffled expression on his face. Donna bent to whisper into his ear. "We're trying to hear what the policeman is saying," she explained, in a voice as soft as the waving of butterfly wings.

"What'd you say?" Bill said. "I can't hear you. Speak up."

Donna sighed, then grabbed Bill's elbow and tugged him off the chair and into the front hallway. When she returned, she was alone. She was carrying Bill's empty plate and fork in her hand.

The women continued to chew in silence until Jane said goodbye to Beau.

"I guess Bill went home?" Grace said to Donna. "Did he get his feelings hurt?"

Donna shrugged. "He didn't understand why we were all so eager to hear what that policeman was saying. So, I told him I'd explain later. Well," she said, turning to look at Jane, "what did he say? I couldn't hear anything."

"He said he just got off the phone with the head of the Gulch Museum's board of directors," Jane said. "Aiden resigned because of a scandal. When he was their director, the museum bought a painting that was supposedly a previously-unknown Bierstadt. It wasn't signed, but Aiden contacted an expert who vouched for it. They found out later it was a fake. The museum had spent a pretty penny on it. If it had been the real thing, it would've been a bargain. And it would've put the Gulch on the map. But, since it's a fake, it can't even be displayed. And there's no way to reclaim their funds."

"How'd they find out it was a fake?" Maisie asked.

"I don't know," Jane said. "But the scandal gets worse. Several of the museum's big donors bought paintings for their own collections from this supposedly newly-discovered find. Again, the paintings were authenticated by Aiden's expert. Now, there are questions about all these works. And, get this: Some people have speculated that Aiden might have been the one who faked them."

"Aiden?" Maisie said. "You mean he was an art forger?"

Jane shrugged. "Nobody has proven it. But, evidently, he was under suspicion - not only for his art advice, but also as a possible forger. That's why the museum got rid of him."

"How come nobody told us about this when we were interviewing candidates?" Grace said. "I'm sure AAC would never have considered hiring him with that kind of stain on his reputation."

"That's why nobody told us," Betsy said. "Gulch wanted him gone, and the best way to get rid of him was to give him a good recommendation."

"Oh, that's just wrong!" Grace said. "It's totally unethical."

"Since when do ethics get in the way of business?" Betsy countered.

Grace exhaled. "Well, you'd think a museum would have some scruples. About art, anyway."

"I suspect they had to keep it hush hush. It would have ruined the Gulch Museum's reputation if the scandal got out," Jane said. "Maybe call into question the integrity of their whole collection."

"Well, I guess it would," Grace said. "And rightfully so."

"But it doesn't add up," Betsy said. "I never saw anything that Aiden painted when he was here. Wouldn't you have to be a really good painter to pull off a forgery?"

"The painting in the hallway of the Gulch Museum is a really good painting," Jane said. "And Honey Pie's work on the Ramblin' Amblin website looks really good. Assuming that Aiden is Honey Pie."

Betsy frowned. "If he was such a good painter, why didn't he ever show off any of his work when he was here?"

"You know, this is fascinating," Maisie said. "All this time, I thought Aiden was just an incompetent person. But it seems like he was a pro." She looked at the women's faces. "Yes, a criminal is a pro. Selling fakes to museums and rich collectors is a major big deal. It would take a lot of expertise. And you can't take classes on art forgery. You have to train yourself."

"It definitely changes my view of him," Pam said. She looked at Jane. "You said he really needed money? To support his brother. And maybe he wasn't going to be able to function much longer if he'd inherited that disease. What'd you call it? Fragile something?"

"Fragile X syndrome. Or some people call it Martin Bell Syndrome," Jane said. "Judging by Aiden's appearance, he probably had the syndrome. Not as severely as his brother. But as he got older, there was a real possibility that he'd develop motor problems. And memory issues."

"Well, I feel sorry for him, what with that medical condition and all. And I certainly admire the way he took care of his brother," Grace said. "But none of that is an excuse for dishonesty."

"The real question is: What does any of this have to do with his murder?" Betsy asked. "Does Strickland think one of the Texas people that Aiden cheated came here and killed him?"

"That's a possibility, isn't it?" Jane said. "All this information changes the nature of the investigation. We may not be looking for a killer motivated by Aiden's incompetent management of a small art center. Lots of money is involved in art forgery. Not to mention a major scandal."

"I notice you said, 'we.'" Maisie chuckled. "You're really into this murder mystery stuff, Jane. The policeman is calling you with new evidence and everything. You've become the Shirley Holmes of Atkinsville!"

"And we decided that I'm her Doc Watson, by the way," Pam said. "I'm going by the pseudonym, Pamson - just for your intel."

Maisie laughed. Which made her snort. And that, of course, started laughter all around.

Betsy stood up. "If we are christening a new name, this calls for a toast." She marched into the kitchen and came back with an open bottle of wine. "Who needs a refill?"

After toasting, the painters stacked up their empty pie plates and chewed over every bit of the news that Beau had delivered. Once every crumb of information had been digested, they drifted back to their easels. The room became quiet, as each painter concentrated on her work.

Jane wet her largest, number 12 brush, doused it in water, and applied a pale yellow wash over her painting's Western sky. Now that the whole sky area was very wet, Jane had a choice: Wait for the paper to dry or work on areas that weren't touching the sky. If she applied a new color and her brush touched the wet area, the new pigment would bleed into the wet area and make the edge blurry. Jane was eager to start painting the focal point, the horse and rider, but Remington had given his figures a crisp, sharp outline against the sky - no blurred edges. So she fished a hairdryer out of her painting supplies and hobbled over to an outlet. As she blew the watercolor paper dry, she thought about Aiden and the art forgery. How did the parts of Aiden's life come together? Did the scandal at his former place of employment bleed into his work at AAC? Or were there clear and distinct edges to each section of his life?

Jane began to mix brown for the horse. With the tip of her brush, she picked up a smear of orange from one of the small cups of color on the sides of her palette. Then she picked up a smear of cobalt and mixed them together in the palette's well. When she tested the resulting brown on a scrap of paper, something struck her as wrong. This was a mousy shade of brown. She frowned. Since the rider and his horse were the focus of her painting, this brown had to be an attractive color, a color that would draw a viewer's eye to the essence of her painting. Her horse's hide didn't have to be an exact match for Remington's, but it did need to accomplish the job of creating a satisfying picture. An ugly shade of brown wouldn't do.

As every painter knows, Jane mused, there are lots of ways to produce brown. Maybe she needed to cool it down? She added a dab of blue-green, but that seemed to accomplish nothing. Maybe this tube had diluted pigment? She squeezed out a larger blob of blue-green and added more to the puddle in the well of her palette. That seemed a little better. But when she tested the color on a scrap of paper, it definitely didn't match the brown in Remington's painting. Nor was it a color that stood out from the browns in the foreground. So, she decided to try the opposite direction and added some red to warm it up. Then she mixed in a little purple to darken it. She tested the color on the horse's flank. Oh, yuck! This color was the opposite of attractive - it reminded her of grease stains.

Jane sat back. She realized her new theory about the murder was just as muddy as the puddle of pigments in the well of her palette. It didn't account for the mystery of the cemetery. Frustrated, she decided to start fresh. She wiped the entire brown puddle off her palette.

Yes, Aiden had a shady history before he came to Atkinsville. And, yes, art forgery was a strong motive for murder. But something about an out-of-town murderer was wrong. How would such a person know about the secret cemetery adjacent to AAC in order to hide the corpse? And anyway, why would a jilted art buyer from Texas follow Aiden all the way to Atkinsville?

Jane sighed. Layering colors took a lot of time and effort, but maybe that was the only way to get the color she needed for the horse. She applied an underpainting of deep purple to the horse to give it a dark undertone. When the purple dried, she'd cover it with a layer of orange. Once that dried, she'd add a layer of cobalt. Since she was using transparent pigments, the lower layers would shine through and blend together in the viewer's eye to produce dark brown. As one of her painting instructors liked to say, it's best to sneak up on the dark areas.

Jane paused, paintbrush in hand. Maybe Aiden had continued to peddle forged art after he moved here to Atkinsville, she thought. And maybe he really did paint his own forgeries to sell. That would explain why he never displayed any of his paintings at AAC. Just because Aiden had moved away from the scandal at the Texas art museum, who's to say he'd given up the racket when he moved here? Beau had said that he'd looked into Aiden's financial records. Jane was sure that he would have noticed if Aiden's bank accounts showed large sums paid to him from out-of-towners. But perhaps somebody local had bought some of Aiden's frauds.

Would Beau have paid attention to a large sum of money from a local source?

No, that still didn't seem right. Jane frowned. If there was somebody in Atkinsville spending megabucks collecting art, surely she would have heard of that person. But it was possible that a rich collector in Atlanta had been cheated by Aiden. That person's motive for the murder would have been a strong one - revenge prompted by the loss of a large sum of money. Jane chewed on the inside of her lip. Would Beau have noticed a money trail from nearby Atlanta?

How could they figure out if Aiden was involved in art forgery when he was living in Atkinsville? Who would know?

Suddenly, the image of a cowboy riding out of the Western sky flashed through Jane's mind. Unlike the cowboy on her painting, this imaginary figure was not the least bit boyish. Nor fully clad. She took out her phone and texted Beau Strickland:

We need to talk to Amblin. She will know if Aiden painted forgeries. And peddled them.

As soon as she sent it, she received his reply:

Amblin comes to settle husband's estate on Friday. Want to meet her?

CHAPTER TWENTY-ONE

"Well, I know this isn't anywhere near as exciting as murder or art forgery," Pam began, as soon as Jane answered her phone, "but I have news. About the gala. Actually, it's not my news - it's Tillie's."

"Huh? What do you mean? Tillie has news?" Jane asked. "Pets aren't allowed at the gala. Are they?"

"Well, Tillie is not just any pet," Pam said. "At least, not anymore. She is Santa's reindeer!"

Pam went on to explain that the gala's organizing committee had decided to end the event with fireworks. As a hilarious touch, Santa would pay a surprise visit as the event was drawing to a close. He'd enter the Old Gym, then shout, 'Ho, Ho, Ho!' to lure the guests outside. As they stood watching, he'd ride away in his sleigh - drawn by reindeer, aka Tillie - as fireworks exploded across the sky.

"Let me guess," Jane said. "Chandler is going to be Santa."

"Of course," Pam said. "He's got a lot of experience in the role."

"But he's too skinny," Jane said. "They really ought to ask somebody else to be Santa. Like Bill. He wouldn't need so much padding around his middle. And he's got the beard."

"Well, I'm not in charge of casting," Pam said. "My job is to get Tillie there. She's the supporting actress."

"You think Tillie is strong enough to pull a cart by herself? With Chandler in it?"

"Well, they're using a golf cart for the sleigh," Pam said. "And it's powered by electricity, so Tillie doesn't have to PULL anything. All she has to do is look reindeer-ish and trot along, with her rein tied to the golf cart."

"Are you going to put antlers on her?" Jane asked.

"Of course," Pam said. She giggled. "What self-respecting reindeer goes bareheaded? And I was thinking of getting her a jingle bell collar."

"I thought Santa had a whole team of reindeer," Jane said.

"Well, duh, that's why they want Tillie for the part," Pam said. "She's big enough to stand in for a whole team of reindeer. Don't you think?"

"Are you going to give her a red nose? Like Rudolph."

"I hadn't thought about it, but that's a great idea," Pam said. "I wonder how I could do that? If I smear anything edible on her nose, she'll lick it right off." She paused. "Hmm, do you think she'd lick off lipstick? They make waterproof lipstick."

Jane started laughing. "This is a totally crazy idea! You're really going to dress Tillie up as a reindeer - that's hilarious! I bet everybody will love it, but it's going to be hard to keep Tillie under control. Don't you think? Especially while everyone's eating."

"She's supposed to be kept secret. Until the end," Pam explained.

"How will you do that? Won't she bark?"

As if on cue, Tillie started barking. Jane heard one loud shrill bark through the phone. Then a crescendo of barking.

"That's a problem," Pam said. "Ruth Alice suggested we could maybe keep her in the Studio Annex until time for her appearance. She can bark her head off out there, and nobody will hear her."

"And you're going to keep this a secret until the gala?" Jane said. "You're not going to tell the other painters?"

"Ruth Alice swore me to secrecy," Pam said. "But I decided I had to tell one person. In case I need help with Tillie, or something. She can be a handful, you know. I thought about telling Betsy because she's got that commanding voice that Tillie really seems to pay attention to. But Betsy can't keep a secret to save her life. And besides, you're the Shirley Holmes of Atkinsville."

"I appreciate the vote of confidence. I guess," Jane said. "I don't have any trouble keeping secrets, but I've never been particularly good at handling Tillie."

"I don't think you'll have anything to worry about," Pam said. "I'll bring Tillie to the Studio Annex early, before anybody arrives for the gala. I'll give her a chew bone or something to keep her busy. When the evening is winding down, Chandler and I will slip out and get everything set up. What could go wrong?"

Hmm. Jane began to picture the evening: The choir singing in sparkling gowns. The Art Angelas dancing in Christmas finery. Men in elegant suits and white shirts. Christmas trees lining the walls, ablaze with glass ornaments reflecting twinkling lights. Tables spread with gleaming platters full of food.... And Tillie. What could possibly go wrong with this picture?

"Okay," Jane said. "If you and the gala committee think you can pull this off, you can count on me as backup. I don't know how I'll be able to help if something goes wrong. But I'll give it my best shot."

As soon as she got off the phone, Jane finished feeding the cats and got in her car to meet Officer Beau Strickland and Amblin. Beau had said that he wanted the meeting to be informal. He thought Amblin would be more likely to divulge useful information if she considered this a friendly conversation, not an official police interview. That's why he'd invited Jane to come along. Plus, he said, Jane knew about more about art than he did.

"You think I know about art forgery!" Jane had exclaimed.

Beau had laughed. "No, I didn't say that. But you know about paints, canvasses, tools. That sort of thing. And painters. I wouldn't know Picasso from Santa Claus. I wouldn't even know where to begin asking questions."

Of course, Jane had agreed to the meeting. After encountering Ramblin' Amblin online, Jane was dying to see her in the flesh. Plus, she was curious about Aiden's life before he'd come to Atkinsville. Although Jane was no expert on art forgery techniques or on Western artists, she probably did know more than Beau. So, she might be able to help by asking questions that would establish a motive for the murder. Maybe even lead to a suspect.

Beau had set the meeting at Christina's at 11 for brunch. That gave Jane two hours before she needed to be at the church for choir rehearsal - the last rehearsal before they performed at the church. After that, the choir would perform their concert one more time - at the AAC gala on Saturday night.

Jane parked in the small lot in front of the cafe. She didn't see a police car, but several cars and a truck were parked. As she approached the cafe door, Cathy Barron opened it from the inside with her hip. She was holding a stack of Styrofoam boxes. Jane hurried to hold the door open for her.

"Thanks, Jane," Cathy said. "Today's our last rehearsal. You ready?"

"I guess. As ready as I'm going to be. Did you just eat lunch here?"

Cathy shook her head. "I'm taking lunch out to Sam. He can't leave. He's the only one at the store today."

As they chatted, Beau Strickland pulled into the parking lot and waved at Jane. When he joined them at the door, Jane said, "Cathy, do you know Officer Beau Strickland? He's with the Atkinsville police."

Beau and Cathy shook hands, and Cathy introduced herself: "Cathy Barron," she said. "I don't think we've met. My husband, Sam, owns that auction barn out on the Billy Barron Road."

Beau nodded. "I know the place."

Cathy studied Beau's face. "Are you from around here? My daughter, Debby, went to high school with a Strickland - Mary Beth Strickland. I remember that her brother was going to police academy."

Nodding, Beau said, "That's me. I remember meeting Debby. Nice girl. Real smart. Went to school up north, I think."

"That's right," Cathy said. "She got her degree from Smith College. Always wanted to go to college in New England. Sam and me, we were so proud of her for getting into an Ivy League school." She rolled her eyes. "That was before we started paying the bills."

"A degree from Smith is quite an accomplishment," Jane said. "I guess she didn't go on a scholarship?"

Cathy shook her head. "No such luck."

"What's she doing now?" Beau asked.

"She's at Yale. Going for a Ph.D in International Studies."

"She must be a great student," Jane said. "I bet she takes after you." Jane looked at Beau. "Cathy was a teacher, you know. Here at the elementary school." She turned to Cathy. "You really must be proud of her."

Cathy beamed. "We are. Well, I better get moving if I'm going to have time to drop off this load and get back in time for rehearsal."

Jane looked around the parking lot. "Are you in your car?"

"No, I took Sam's truck. He needed me to pick up that stuff." Cathy pointed to a truck with a load of furniture in its cargo bed. Jane saw an old-fashioned piano, several chairs, and various pieces of what seemed like heavy antique furniture.

"I guess somebody died?" Jane said. "And their children are selling off the estate?"

"Actually, no," Cathy said. "Downsizing. Moving to a subdivision. Family was living way out on the far side of the county. On land that used to be a peach orchard. Sort of a shame that they're selling. Place was in the family for generations." She looked at Jane. "Maybe you know them? Andy Harrison. He's a doctor. Wife's active at AAC."

"That's the orthopedic doctor that I saw about my ankle," Jane said. "I wonder why he's giving up his family estate. If it's a big place, I'm sure the upkeep is expensive. But doctors make oodles of money."

Cathy shrugged. "His wife told me they got tired of living way out there. It's a long drive into town. They have three school-age kids, and I guess it gets old - always having to shuttle the kids back and forth to sports and all. Plus, that's a lot of acreage to take care of. Big old house - I'm sure it was constantly in need of something. Painting, repairs. I know they had a major problem with the roof last year. Just because your family lived in the country for years and years, doesn't mean you have to like living out there." Cathy smiled. "Well, speaking of a long drive - I really better get going. Nice to meet you, Beau. I'll tell Debby that I saw you. See you at rehearsal, Jane."

CHAPTER TWENTY-TWO

Jane and Beau went inside. Seated at a table near the wall, with her back to the door, was a woman wearing a bright yellow sweater and jeans. Around her neck was a red bandanna, and silver hoop earrings dangled on each side of her ponytail. As they approached the table, the woman swiveled, and Jane recognized Ramblin' Amblin's face - as well as her style. Amblin's vee-neck sweater was skin tight, and its vee dipped nearly all the way to the large leather belt that clinched her waistband.

"Amblin?" Beau said, approaching the table. He smiled. "I'm Officer Beau Strickland. Call me Beau."

Jane stuck out her hand to shake Amblin's. "Glad to meet you, I'm Jane Roland," she said. "I've seen your work on your website. I'm a painter, too." Jane slid onto the bench beside Beau. "This must be a difficult trip for you, Amblin - what with Aiden's death and the unusual circumstances. I'm sorry for your loss."

Amblin shrugged. "Are you?"

After that awkward introduction, Amblin informed them that she was only going to be in Atkinsville for the day. She'd flown in the night before. "I'm meeting with the lawyer as soon as we're done here. To sign all the papers," she said. "Then I'm heading out of Dodge. I've got a motel near the airport, and I fly back to Chicago in the morning."

"That's a quick turnaround. Are you planning to go out to Aiden's house?" Beau asked. "I should warn you that it's surrounded by police tape. So, if you have any items to pick up...."

Amblin waved her hand as she interrupted him: "There's nothing there that I give a hoot about."

"Are you sure?" Beau asked. "I could...."

"I figure I ditched near about 150 pounds when I ditched Aiden," Amblin said. "No way I'm putting any of his baggage back in my saddlebags. Whatever he kept in his redneck shack doesn't interest me - not one bit."

"Are you planning to hire a real estate agent to sell the place?" Jane asked. She glanced at Beau. "When the police are through with it, I could suggest a few names of local agents. And arrange for someone to come and empty out the house for you."

"No thanks," Amblin said, waving her hand again. "Got me an agent on the internet. I told him to sell whatever he finds in that dump. Or burn it. Just get rid of it.'"

Jane thought it was a relief when the uncomfortable conversation had to pause for them to look over the brunch menu. Jane already knew what she wanted - the veggie egg white scramble, with a side of sweet potato fries. As she waited for the others to decide, she studied Amblin. The woman was a difficult person to get to know, Jane thought. Or like. But if they were going to learn anything useful from her, Jane would have to figure out how to charm her way past Amblin's prickly exterior.

After they ordered, Jane introduced a new topic. "Officer Strickland tells me that you're donating all of the profits from the sale of Aiden's house to his disabled brother. I admire your generosity."

"Do you?" Amblin said. "Way I look at it, it's another 150 pounds out of my saddlebags."

Topics related to Aiden and his brother seemed to be getting them nowhere. So Jane decided to try art. Maybe, if she flattered Amblin? "I enjoyed exploring your website," Jane began. "I paint in watercolor, and my paintings tend to be airy, delicate. I'm intrigued by your vivid colors. And your approach to your subjects is, um, bold. Direct. Refreshing, really. You don't hold anything back."

Amblin laughed. "That's one way to put it. Tell you the truth, women don't usually go for my work." She shrugged again.

As she chewed on a fry, Jane glanced at Beau. He didn't give any indication that he was going to jump onto this horse. "Actually, I noticed two distinct styles on your website," Jane continued. "Some of the paintings were by Honey Pie. Are those yours, too?"

"Nah, Aiden did them. Back when we were together," Amblin said. "I guess I ought to take them down, but I don't know what to do with them. If he hadn't gotten himself into such a mess at the Gulch, I could donate them. They might have been worth something. Once. Not anymore."

Finally! Amblin had opened the door to a discussion of Aiden's cloudy past. Jane rushed in. "I heard about that - the scandal with a painting that the Gulch purchased. It was supposedly a Bierstadt, wasn't it?"

Amblin looked at Jane. "Why are you here? Are you a policeman?"

Jane swallowed and looked at Beau. "No. I'm just a ... a friend of Officer Strickland, here. He knows I'm interested in art. So...."

"I invited Jane along because I'm not real familiar with paintings," Beau said. "And I knew Aiden had gotten mixed up in some business with art forgery when he was at the Gulch Museum. In a murder investigation, everything is relevant. I don't know if that incident might have anything to do with the way Aiden died."

"You're thinking somebody from the art museum up and killed him?" Amblin exclaimed. She snorted. "Not hardly! I grant you, Aiden never should have listened to that art dealer. My husband was a fool, that's all. What are the chances that an undiscovered Bierstadt would be found? Or offered to little ole Aiden Parson - rather than some art bigwig in New York or L.A.?"

"Well, he was the director of a museum that specialized in Western art," Jane said.

"The Gulch is just a small prairie dog in the art world," Amblin said. "Not like one of them big city museums. The Gulch doesn't have the bankroll. Or the experts. Aiden was a patsy. He got conned, that's all. The Gulch should have known better than to trust his recommendation."

"But Aiden must have had some expertise in Western art. I've seen the mural that he did," Jane said, "in the hallway of the museum. His work looks a lot like the masters of Western art."

Amblin didn't react, so Jane continued: "I understand that some people have speculated that Aiden painted the forged Bierstadt himself. And that several private collectors also bought Bierstadt paintings from the same alleged find. So they're probably fakes, too. Maybe forgeries that Aiden produced. All this must have made some very powerful people angry. Very angry."

"Yeah, they were mad," Amblin said. "Served them right. They thought they could bypass the legit dealers and rope themselves a bargain. A real Bierstadt for their big, fancy ranch houses. Something to impress their rich friends. Well, that's not the way the world works. You get what you pay for. If something's too good to be true, it's probably not true. That's all there is to it."

Beau leaned forward and asked, "Well, did he?"

"Did who? What?"

"Aiden. Did he paint the fake Beer-somethings?" Beau asked.

Amblin grimaced. "Aiden? Paint a fake Bierstadt? No way." She looked at Jane. "You said you're a painter. You've seen Honey Pie's paintings. They look like Remingtons. But Bierstadt? Not on your life."

Beau frowned. "It's Aiden's life that I'm thinking about," he said. "I'm thinking he got in over his head, and it might have cost him his life. This is important: Did your husband ever create a forged painting and sell it?"

Amblin scowled. She pursed her lips together. Jane wondered if Beau had pushed her too far, and she would refuse to say anything else.

"Look. Nobody is accusing you of forgery. Or anything underhanded," Jane said. "But I believe you told Officer Strickland, here, that you'd figured out how to make an honest living - now that Aiden is no longer in the picture. What did you mean by that? It sounds like Aiden was making a dishonest living."

Jane thought Amblin's cheeks were turning red. The woman squirmed.

"Okay, I'm not saying Aiden had the morals of a priest," Amblin said. "Yes, he got a finder's fee for the Bierstadts. A nice finder's fee. And he knew good and well that he should've sent the paintings off to be evaluated by an expert. But he thought he knew enough to examine a painting for evidence of forgery. Consulting an expert is expensive. And time consuming. The dealer wasn't going to wait around forever; he was pressuring Aiden. "

"So you're saying that Aiden vouched for the dealer, even though he had his suspicions," Beau said. "Aiden wanted the money. And the dealer turned out to be a scumbag."

Amblin nodded. "Yup, you got it."

"I'll need the name and contact of this dealer," Beau said. He slid his pad and pen across the table.

Amblin picked up the pen. "I guarantee you won't find him at this address anymore," she said as she jotted some words on Beau's pad. "Or with this name."

Beau nodded. "It's a place to start."

"And you're saying Aiden imitated the style of some of the classic Western painters. But he wasn't an art forger," Jane said. "His only crime - if you could call it a crime - was neglecting to have the Bierstadts authenticated. Even though he knew better."

"That's right," Amblin said, as she stood up. "My ex was no angel, but he wasn't a criminal. He needed money, and an opportunity came his way. It was only a matter of time before his painting days were over, and he knew it. He had that idiot brother to support. Believe me, Aiden wasn't exactly raking in the big bucks working at some dinky little art museum. So he took a gamble."

"And his gamble lost him his good name," Jane said. "And his wife?"

"I don't know if it lost him his good name," Amblin said. "Y'all hired him, didn't you?"

"But it cost him his wife?" Jane asked again.

Amblin snorted. "You ever been out to Texas Hill Country? You better believe his wife started packing her bags as soon as he decided to move to that godforsaken place."

As soon as Amblin left, Jane looked at Beau. "Well? What do you think? Do you believe what she said? That Aiden wasn't an art forger - just an opportunist? A guy who had a chance to make some quick money and fell for a scam?"

Beau looked like he was chewing on his answer. He popped his last fry into his mouth, then wadded up his paper napkin and dropped it on top of the soiled waxed paper lining his basket. "She could have been lying to protect herself," he said. "If Aiden did forge all those beer paintings... What'd you call them?"

"Not beer. Bierstadt," Jane said. She spelled the name. "Albert Bierstadt. He painted Western landscapes."

"Ah," Beau nodded.

"It's true that Aiden's work didn't look anything like Bierstadt's style," Jane said. "Aiden painted cowboys, horses, indigenous people. Paintings that look like posters for Hollywood movies. At least, that's the style of the paintings by Honey Pie on Amblin's website. And the mural he painted for the Gulch Museum."

Beau picked up Jane's empty basket and piled it on top of his own. "Yes," he said.

"Yes?" Jane asked.

"Yes, I do believe Amblin. I think a shady art dealer offered some fakes to Aiden, and he was the perfect patsy. New at the job. Out-of-the-way museum. No experience authenticating art. Aiden should have known better, but he saw a chance to make some easy money, and he took it."

"Are you going to follow up on the art dealer?"

Beau nodded. "Guess so. But I don't think it'll get me anywhere."

"Are you thinking the forged paintings had something to do with Aiden's murder?" Jane asked.

Beau frowned.

"Because that leaves the question of the cemetery," Jane said. "Means, motive, and opportunity - isn't that the formula for crime? The forgery could provide the motive for Aiden's murder. Anybody could have hit him on the head - that's the means. But how do you account for opportunity? Stuffing his body into a casket in a cemetery that nobody knew about?"

Beau stood and gathered up the dirty baskets to bus them to the trash. He chuckled. "You know, you're really something," he said. "Ruth Alice said they call you Shirley at the art center. For Shirley Holmes. And they think you're going to write a mystery novel about solving crimes. You going to write about Aiden's murder?"

"Depends."

"On what?" Beau asked as he opened the door to the parking lot for Jane.

"On whether we figure out whodunnit."

CHAPTER TWENTY-THREE

When her minuet ringtone rang out, Jane grabbed a dishtowel and wiped her hands. Betsy's face was on the screen of her phone.

"Hi," Jane said. "I'm getting the buckeyes packed now. When do you want to come by?"

Jane had been packing her homemade "buckeyes" - chocolate-covered peanut butter balls - on layers of wax paper inside two plastic tubs that had once held caramel popcorn. Although the banquet at the AAC gala was always catered by a local restaurant, the desserts were contributed by members. If previous galas were any indication, the dessert buffet would overflow with sugary delights - fluffy pecan pralines, slices of buttery pound cake, and creamy fudge from treasured family recipes.

Each year, Jane volunteered to make her buckeyes. When she was a child, her mom made the candies every Christmas, and the memory was a cherished part of Jane's holidays. She'd spent all day yesterday mixing up the peanut butter middles, then dunking each ball in chocolate and laying the round candies on trays to dry.

"I'll come now - if you're ready," Betsy said. She'd volunteered to pick up Jane's contribution to the dessert buffet and take it to AAC, so Jane wouldn't have to figure out how to carry the containers while maneuvering on her crutches. "My shortbread bars are all boxed up. After I drop off the desserts at AAC, I'm going to come back home to shower. Jim and I could pick you up later and give you a ride over, if you want?"

"No, thanks. The choir's supposed to arrive early. I shouldn't have any problem driving myself. Especially with you taking the buckeyes over for me," Jane said. She paused. "Betsy, would you happen to have any extra trays? Something pretty that we could set out on the table? I was going to display the buckeyes in my long white casserole pan, but I can't find it. I've looked everywhere. I must have taken it to somebody's house and forgotten it."

"I have a big lasagna pan. It's red, so it'll match the holiday theme. I think it'll hold a couple dozen buckeyes. Want to use that?"

"If you don't mind," Jane said.

"Only thing is, I need the pan tomorrow," Betsy said. "We're having a potluck at church, and I signed up for lasagna. You know that recipe I make - with sausage?"

"Shouldn't be a problem." Jane said. "I can give you the pan tonight. Just don't let me forget."

"Okay. I'm going to leave now. I should be at your house in a few."

While she finished piling buckeyes on the top layers, Jane sang a few of the numbers in the Christmas concert. Although the choir performance at church had gone without a hitch, there were more than a dozen song lyrics to keep in mind. As usual, Jane was feeling a prickle of pre-performance nerves. She'd be singing to a packed house tonight at the AAC gala. And the audience would be friends and fellow artists. She didn't want to mess up in front of all those people.

The sound of the doorbell interrupted her solo concert. At the door, Betsy showed her the lasagna pan.

"That should be perfect," Jane said.

"Did you hear?" Betsy announced, as she marched into the kitchen. "It's a sell-out! The Old Gym's at capacity. There are no tickets to sell at the door."

"Wow! That's a first, isn't it?" Jane said. "They've done great advertising this year. I think those social media posts that Ruth Alice created were really effective. I've seen at least half a dozen posts on Facebook. Don't you think that's the reason they've sold so many tickets?"

Betsy laughed. "Nope. I think it's the rumors."

"Rumors? What do you mean?" Jane asked. "You talking about Aiden's murder and the cemetery? Seems like that would keep people away - not attract them. It makes AAC seem like a sinister place."

"No, not that. I mean the rumors about a visit from the Jolly Old Elf," Betsy said.

"Oh, I didn't hear about that," Jane lied. Had somebody spilled the beans to Betsy about Chandler appearing as Santa, with Tillie as his reindeer? "What surprise visit?"

"I can't tell you," Betsy said with a smirk. "Sworn to secrecy. Scout's honor. Cross my heart and hope to die. Let's just say that this year's gala is going to end with a bang. It will be - as they say in Paree - a *denouement* to *souvien!*"

After Betsy left, Jane hurried upstairs to shower and dress. The cats were waiting at the foot of the stairs when she came down. They reminded her - loud and clear - that they wanted their evening treats before she left. On the way out the door, she flipped on the front porch light. She wasn't expecting to be home from the gala until well past nine.

Although Jane pulled into the AAC parking lot about 45 minutes early, the only open spots were in front of the Studio Annex. Fortunately, it was an easy enough walk across the road to the Old Gym. While she swung her crutches out of the trunk, she gave a sigh of relief that she hadn't arrived any later - the overflow parking was on a grassy field, and after the rain earlier in the week, the field would be muddy and awkward to maneuver with crutches. She dropped her keys into a small purse that she could carry with a wristband. Then she draped a long red cashmere shawl around her shoulders. It was going to be a chilly night - perfect weather for a holiday gala.

Tall, slim evergreens in buckets lined the short walkway leading up to the Old Gym. The trees were covered in strings of clear, twinkly lights. Even though it was barely dusk, Jane thought the effect was magical - like walking through a miniature lane into a land of enchantment. At the door, Jane paused to admire the decorations inside. False walls covered with thick wreaths narrowed the hallway into a sort of leafy green tunnel. As Jane emerged from the hallway into the basketball court, she glanced up at enormous scallops of green, draped like vines in a jungle, hanging from the overhead beams. The room smelled like pine needles and cinnamon.

At the far end, against the back wall, Jane saw the dessert buffet - four banquet tables covered in golden cloths. She headed for the tables, which were resplendent with gleaming silver trays and shiny platters. There were fluffy coconut cakes that reminded Jane of snow sculptures. Magnificent red velvet cakes perched on footed plates. She noted that Betsy had already set out the buckeyes, and the shiny chocolate balls gleamed like little moons in the red lasagna pan. Scanning the table, Jane spotted Betsy's shortbread squares and the bite-sized key lime cheesecakes that Pam always made. Jane couldn't help grinning at what looked like a parade of chocolate mice, with long peppermint tails, arranged artfully as if they were creeping across the front of one of the tables.

Filling the center of the big room were enormous, round banquet tables, covered with floor-length white cloths. Each table had a potted poinsettia as a centerpiece. The pots were surrounded by blown-glass ornaments, one for each guest to take home as a memento. A hand-lettered table number, affixed to a stick, poked out of each pot.

Jane checked her ticket, found her table number, and deposited her purse and shawl at one of the table's 10 place settings. She glanced down at two biodegradable plastic glasses standing beside a recyclable bamboo plate full of green salad. The tableware made Jane cringe. It looked tacky - completely out of keeping with the rich, bountiful decor adorning the walls and ceiling. But after the collapse of the old bomb shelter and the destruction of all the center's glassware, the gala committee had sensibly decided that disposable tableware was a more practical solution. Ugh, Jane thought. Disposable plates simply don't give off the same ambience as the real glass dishes that they'd used at previous galas. Jane shrugged and told herself to get over it. After all, these were just plates and glasses - destined to get soiled with food and drink. They were there to fulfill a function, not to decorate. Besides, at the end of the evening, this tableware could be thrown in the recycling bin. It would be a relief for Jane, as well as the other volunteers, who wouldn't have to schlep boxes of glassware that needed to be run through a dishwasher.

Some of the other choir members were already gathered at the side of the room in front of the bleachers. They'd use these as risers for their performance. Smiling, Jane waved at Cathy Barron, who was chatting with her husband Sam. After Jane found a corner to store her crutches, she hobbled over. Cathy and Sam each held one of Jane's elbows to help her clamber up two bleachers into her singing position. Then Sam kissed Cathy on her cheek, wished them both good luck, and jumped off the makeshift stage.

"What do you think of that row of potted trees in front of the building?" Cathy asked Jane.

"I love the effect," Jane said. "It was magical. Like walking into Narnia. Whose idea was it?"

"Brianna McClary. She's one of the new Angelas. They own McClary's Nursery. You know - that place on Highway 552. On the way to Sam's auction barn."

"I don't think I've met her," Jane said.

"They moved here last year. They're friends of Ed Walker. You know - the attorney on the board."

Jane nodded. Of course, she knew Ed. He'd been dating Grace. "Ed seems to bring a lot of people to AAC. I think he's the one who originally encouraged Aiden to apply for the director's job." Jane looked at the vines hanging down from the ceiling. "Seems like the McClarys will be more of an asset than Aiden ever was. Did their nursery supply all this greenery, too?"

Cathy nodded. "Yes, everything. The trees, the wreaths in the hall, and these big vines."

"Wow! These are by far the best decorations we've ever had," Jane said. "Must have cost AAC a pretty penny."

"What I hear, the McClarys donated all of it. Had their people come out and set it up, too."

"Impressive," Jane said. She made a mental note to mention the nursery's name to Beau. Also, to ask him if he'd found out anything about Ed Walker. Follow the money trails - that's what they always said in detective movies.

The choir director bustled over, an excited smile on his face. "Ready?" he said. He glanced around. The room was filling with people. Men and women in holiday finery were standing in clumps, greeting and mingling. Jane could feel her skin tingling with anticipation.

"The acoustics in this building are very different than the church," the choir director reminded them. "In here, we have to give it our all. Let our voices ring out. Fill the air with glorious sound."

As soon as all the singers were in their places on the bleachers, the director raised his arms to lead them in their typical holiday warmup: "We Wish You a Merry Christmas."

Around the room, people looked up and smiled. They began sliding into seats at the round tables.

After the song, the choir director spun around, picked up the handheld microphone, and invited the audience to join the choir in a familiar song: "The Twelve Days of Christmas."

"At your tables," he said, "you'll find the words printed on your programs. In case you need a refresher." He turned to face the choir members and smiled. "Here we go. Let's make this a night to remember!"

After the whole roomful sang "The Twelve Days of Christmas," the director announced: "Now, relax and sit back. It's our turn to give you the gift of song. Let the season of joy begin!"

The director swiveled to face the choir, and they burst into the first of the numbers in their program. Jane smiled at Cathy, standing next to her, as her voice lifted to blend into the gorgeous collage of sound. This was the high point of her holiday season, Jane reflected. The culmination of her year. Here she was, surrounded by wonderful friends in this delightful art center. It had been an eventful year for both her and AAC. In spring, she'd survived a terrifying art retreat with a murderer in their midst. In autumn, she'd survived a terrifying cave-in, with a broken ankle. The art center, itself, had been shadowed by mystery, tragedy. But tonight, all that was behind them. Jane felt that every word of every song was a celebration of life, of renewal, of creativity.

The entire chorus seemed to echo her emotion. They sang as if the power and majesty of the holidays had entered into their voices. Jane was sure they'd never performed so well. And the audience seemed to agree. After the last number, after the choir took their bows, the audience rose as one entity. Applause thundered across the room. The choir began their pre-arranged "extra" song, in response to the ovation. Afterward, the audience rose again, and again the choir responded with song. After the third ovation, they'd run out of songs, and - tired but delighted - the choir took their final bow.

The chorus members descended from the bleachers and began filing across the room to their tables. Cathy and the choir director each took one of Jane's arms to help her down. Ruth Alice was standing on the floor, waiting to congratulate them.

"That was astounding," Ruth Alice gushed. "You could have been performing at the Lincoln Center. It was that good." She kissed the choir director's cheek and gave Jane a big hug.

Jane collected her crutches and moved across the room, stopping to accept accolades from friends. Chandler, seated at a table with several of the Angelas, lifted his hands to his lips and blew her a dramatic kiss. At another table, Jane spotted Andy Harrison, her orthopedic doctor, seated beside his wife. Andy was wearing his silly, red and green striped, blinking-light bowtie. As Jane pushed by on her crutches, he yelled, "Bravo!"

When Jane reached her own table, Pam stood and took the crutches, then helped her get settled. "Great job," Pam said. "I think that was your best concert, ever."

Donna, who was sitting beside Bill across the table, leaned forward. "You sounded really really good," she said. "I guess that's the reason they say, 'break a leg,' before a performance. Breaking your leg - or your ankle - must improve your voice."

"I don't know about that." Jane smiled. "But I do know that it makes it inconvenient to climb up on bleachers."

Bill picked up his wineglass and began to tap it with a fork. When he had the attention of everybody at their table, he rose, flourishing a bottle of champagne, and looked at Jane. "Here's to you," he announced. "Our own little Maria Callas!" He grabbed the bottle by the neck, and - with a dramatic gesture - uncorked it. As champagne bubbled out, Donna stuck a glass under the flow.

When all their glasses were full, they toasted: "To Jane!"

Beaming, Jane decided that plastic wine glasses weren't so tacky after all.

As she put down her glass, Pam said to Bill, "You know, you really had me going, for a minute. The way you whipped out that bottle, I thought you were going to hurl it across the room."

Donna gave her funny little "heh, heh" chuckle. "You mean, like that guy you bought the chandelier from? What was his name, again?"

"Tony Keller," Pam said.

Jane shook her head, remembering. "How could we forget him? The guy who claimed AAC had stolen his painting."

"I guess it's always a shame to lose a membership," Grace said. "But I'm just as glad that man won't be coming to any more events here."

The rest of the evening passed in a sparkle of conversation, food and drink, dancing, and party games. Everybody seemed to love the dinner, which was served by a cadre of students from the local high school's art club. The dessert buffet received raves all around and multiple visits from most.

Toward the end of the evening, Pam returned to the table, her arms full of empty containers. Along with her silver trays, she was holding Jane's plastic tubs and Betsy's lasagna pan. "Your buckeyes were quite the hit," Pam said. "There aren't but a handful left. They've put the last few in with the cookies."

Jane reached for her empty containers, but Pam moved them out of her reach. "Don't be silly. You can't carry these with crutches," Pam said. "Where are you parked?"

"By the Studio Annex."

"I'll take them out for you," Pam said. She winked. "There's a certain matter that I need to attend to out there." She cleared her throat dramatically. Then she leaned close to Jane and whispered, "Cover for me, will you, if anybody asks where I've gone."

"I promised Betsy that I'd give her the pan tonight," Jane said. "She needs it for a potluck at her church tomorrow."

"Not to worry," Pam said. "I'll put it in your car." She got up and walked briskly toward the hallway. Jane watched Chandler join Pam, and the two slipped out the door.

As soon as they were gone, Ruth Alice picked up the microphone and cleared her throat to get everybody's attention. "Hasn't this been an amazing evening!" she gushed. She called out the names of the gala committee members, and everybody applauded. Then she thanked the chorus, the dessert makers, the servers, McClary's Nursery, and a long list of other sponsors. She reminded everyone to take home one of the glass ornaments at the table as a gift from AAC.

At the end of the announcements, Ruth Alice stopped and curled a hand around one ear, as if to listen. "Did you hear what I hear?" she sang out. "No, it's not a child singing in the night. It's .... It's .... Why, it's the Jolly Ole Elf, himself!"

At that moment, Chandler - in full Santa regalia - burst out of the hallway, shouting "Ho, Ho, Ho!" As soon as he'd caught everybody's attention, he beckoned for them to follow him. "To the rooftop!" he called and disappeared into the greenery.

Ruth Alice announced, "Looks like Santa's got a surprise for us. Grab your coats, folks - it's a frosty night - and let's go watch Ole Saint Nick's departure for his legendary trip around the world."

A human flood rushed through the hall behind Ruth Alice, washed out the door, and spilled into the chilly night. And there, on the road, was Santa in a golf cart festooned with blinking, colored lights. Sitting beside him on the seat was Tillie the reindeer, antlers askew on her big square head, licking furiously at her red-lipsticked nose. As the golf cart began to glide away, fireworks exploded in the sky above them and illuminated the field with glorious colors.

CHAPTER TWENTY-FOUR

Jane felt herself getting goosebumps as the dazzling bursts of sound and color peppered the air above AAC. The vast darkness became a shifting canvas of light and smoke. Clasping her shawl around her shoulders, she shivered. Hmm, she thought - perhaps her goosebumps were not so much a reaction to the beauty as to the cold. Although she was surrounded by a dense knot of people, the wind seemed to whip through the throng of bodies and penetrate her clothing.

A final rocket streaked into the sky, forming a tall green stalk. It rose straight up and opened into a huge, flaming red flower.

"Look - a poinsettia!" Donna exclaimed. "Well, that was quite the dramatic finish to the evening!"

"Wasn't it, though!" said Grace. She was standing on Donna's other side, with Ed Walker beside her.

"A truly artistic finale!" Ed said. "By the way, do you know whose dog that was in the cart with Chandler? Dressed up as a reindeer?"

"Pam's, I think. Wasn't it?" Bill chuckled and shook his head. "If that wasn't the fattest, laziest reindeer I ever saw!"

Betsy and her husband Jim pushed through the crowd. Jim, who was a dedicated photographer, was holding his large, professional camera. He shifted from foot to foot, looking uncomfortably chilly. No wonder, Jane thought. He didn't have a jacket, and he was wearing the thin guayabera shirt that he'd brought back from their last tropical vacation. Betsy, in a long embroidered sweater, seemed better prepared for the weather. In her arms, she was holding a stack of empty trays.

"Well, I predicted it was going to be an unforgettable ending, didn't I?" Betsy said to Jane.

"Oh, so you knew about this?" Grace said. "I don't remember hearing anything about it."

"It was supposed to be a secret," Jane said. "Only the gala committee and the actors knew. Pam told me - in case she needed someone to help with Tillie. But she swore me to secrecy."

"Well, I might have heard about it from a little elf on the committee," Betsy said. "Who happens to go to our church. And wanted Jim to take some photos of the fireworks for AAC's website."

"Did you get any good shots?" Ed asked him.

"I think so," Jim said. "Brr. Awfully cold tonight, isn't it? I don't remember them predicting this frosty snap." He looked at Betsy. "I'm going to go turn on the car. Get the heater started. See y'all later," he said as he headed across the road toward the field.

"Be right along," Betsy called after him. She turned to Jane. "Hey, I didn't see my lasagna pan on the buffet table. Did you pick it up?"

"Pam took it. She didn't want me to have to carry the containers with my crutches." Jane said.

Betsy grimaced.

"I know you need it for tomorrow. Tell you what," Jane said, "you go on. I'll find Pam and bring the pan by your house on my way home."

"Okay," Betsy said. "Just call when you get to the house. I'll come out so you don't have to get out of the car."

The crowd was dispersing as Jane took out her phone and texted Pam: Where r u? Betsy needs red pan. She tucked her phone into the little purse around her wrist and started maneuvering on her crutches toward the lot in front of the Studio Annex. She tried to stay close to the edge of the road because cars were pulling out.

One car stopped beside her, and Donna rolled down her window. "Want a ride to your car?"

Jane shook her head. "I'm almost there. But thanks."

As she plodded up the slight rise, Jane felt her phone buzz. She stopped to read the screen: Red pan in Annex with my stuff. Ur car was locked.

Stopping by her car, Jane unlocked the door and fished out a reusable shopping bag. She could slip the handles over her shoulder to carry all the containers. Pushing her crutches along the narrow walkway, she made her way up to the Studio Annex. The building was dark and looked deserted. As she reached the door, the motion sensor lights switched on, and Jane entered the code to let herself in. She used the flashlight on her phone to guide her to the drawing classroom. At the doorway, she turned on the overhead fluorescent lights and looked around the room. Betsy's pan and the other containers were nowhere in sight. Maybe Pam had deposited them on the floor behind the teacher's desk?

As she pushed her crutches around tables, Jane almost tripped on something sticking out of the art supply closet. The door to the closet was ajar, and the light was on. Opening the door, Jane saw a painting on the floor, propped against the door jamb. Why in the world had someone left a painting here? Afraid she might have damaged it, Jane leaned over to look. It was a landscape, probably an oil, on a wood panel. The painting was nice enough - typical forest scene, with leafy trees, a thin stream, and a few rocks. She picked it up. It was unusually heavy. Most of the weight seemed to be the gold frame, which was extraordinary. It looked old-fashioned - wide and thick, with beading around the inner edge and elaborate swirls around the rest. She gave a sigh of relief that there were no nicks on the painting or damage to the frame. But she didn't want to put it back where it was - in harm's way. Surely, somebody must have left it here by accident? Who did it belong to? Shining her phone's flashlight over the surface, Jane looked for a signature. She didn't see anything in the lower right, where most painters signed their work. But in the lower left corner, she found two thin initials in tan paint: T. K.

That's odd, Jane thought. She couldn't think of any artist at the center with those initials. She turned the painting over, hoping to find a slip of paper taped to the back. At AAC exhibits, artists taped an identification form - with their names and the titles of their work - to the back of their artwork. But instead of a piece of paper, Jane discovered another painting on the reverse side of the wood panel!

Tucking the painting under her arm, Jane backed out of the closet so she could examine it in the brighter classroom. Whatever was painted on the reverse side was very dark. It was hard to see details. Shining her phone's flashlight over it, Jane could make out three tiny figures seated on what looked like a blanket. Dark shapes, probably foliage and mountains, formed the backdrop. The painting seemed really old. In a few spots, the paint was actually cracked and flaking. But in the lower right corner, there seemed to be a light area. It looked like somebody had swiped off some of the dirt to reveal a signature. Jane didn't have her reading glasses, so she held the painting close to her face and squinted, trying to make out the name.

Suddenly, the room went dark! Jane felt her legs give way as her crutches were pulled out from under her, and something slammed against the orthopedic boot supporting her injured ankle. Pain shot through her leg. She could feel herself falling! She gasped as she was whipped around, and a cloth - was it a blanket? her red shawl? - was wound tightly around her head and arms. The wool squeezed against her nose and mouth, making it hard to breathe. She felt herself being dragged and shoved. Then her head collided against something hard.

When she came to, Jane was lying in a heap on a cold, hard surface. Her head throbbed. She was freezing. She twisted and squirmed until she managed to loosen the shawl and free her fingers. Where was she? It was pitch black, and she couldn't see anything, but she could feel a gritty wood floor underneath her. She tried to sit up, but her head hit something. Ouch! A shelf? Was she in the closet? The narrow closet in the drawing classroom? It smelled of dust and wood, paint and chemicals. A tingle of fear crawled up her back. Somebody had pushed her in here. Why? What was going on?

Slowly, Jane squirmed out from under the shelf and sat up. She tried to get her bearings. From the shape and size of her surroundings, she decided she must be in the art supply closet. The door was closed, and there was no light coming in from the classroom. Sliding on her butt, she inched forward and felt for the door knob. It twisted, but she couldn't make the door budge. Something heavy must be wedging it shut on the other side. She was trapped! Her first impulse was to scream. But she stifled the urge. Somebody had put her in here. By now, all the gala attendees must have gone home, and the AAC campus would be empty. If somebody meant to do her harm, screaming wouldn't help. Should she switch on the closet light? Whoever had pushed her in here might be able to see the light under the door. Maybe it was better to pretend that she was still unconscious? Quietly, she began to grope around the floor, hoping to find her phone. No luck.

Jane could hear muffled voices on the other side of the door. Men's voices. She leaned closer to listen. Were there two of them? There didn't seem to be any light in the classroom. So whoever was in there didn't want to be seen by anybody passing by.

"You sure?" one of the voices said.

"I saw her. She was shining a light right on it."

"Doesn't mean she saw it." The voice sounded annoyed. "And even if she did, she wouldn't get what it means."

That voice sounded familiar, but Jane couldn't identify it. She pushed against the door, trying to enlarge the crack so she could hear better.

The other voice sounded tense, angry. "I'm telling you, somebody will recognize it. That damn fool Tony made such a big deal of it."

Tony! Like a flash of lightning, Jane put it together: The signature on the landscape, T.K. The initials stood for Tony Keller - the man who'd hurled the wine bottle at the opening reception for the Santa Store. The painting on the floor must have been his "stolen" painting. But what was it doing in the closet? Jane strained to listen. Was Tony Keller one of the men out there? She'd only heard his voice a few times, but she didn't think either of the men sounded like him.

"This is how we got into this mess," the first voice hissed. "If you'd stop and think before you .... Look, there's no way out of it, now. I'm going to call the police."

"No!" The other voice shouted. And then, quieter, but insistent: "I'm telling you she'll figure it out. Cathy says she's some kind of Sherlock Holmes. As soon as they make the connection with the painting, somebody's going to figure out the rest."

Jane's head started spinning. The watercolor painters called her Shirley Holmes, but what men knew about the nickname? Chandler. Beau Strickland. Maybe one of the painter's husbands? Ed Walker, the man who was dating Grace. But that voice had said Cathy. Cathy who? The only Cathy she knew was Cathy Barron.

"I don't think so," the calmer voice was saying. "We can say we came in here to get something and found her. Unconscious. That we interrupted a robbery. Woman alone in the building. Somebody tried to snatch her wallet. We'll be the ones who came to her rescue. You said she didn't see you. She's going to be fuzzy on the details, anyway. You knocked her out - she's probably got a concussion."

That word - "concussion" - sounded familiar. Jane had heard a voice saying that word. Suddenly, it came to her: It was the voice of her orthopedic doctor - Andy Harrison!

"I don't want to risk it," said the other voice. "I say we make her disappear. You're a doctor - you can do it. Make it look like she had an aneurysm or something. Because of the broken bone."

Disappear! Was he suggesting that they kill her? Jane's mouth went dry. Her heart was beating so loud that she was afraid they could hear it. What should she do? She raised herself on one knee and ran her hands over the shelf. There must be something in here that she could use as a weapon. She had to be careful not to make any noise - not to knock anything off the shelf. She couldn't let them know that she was awake, listening. Her fingers felt a slim shaft of wood. A hammer! She pulled it off the shelf.

"I don't know how to do that. I'm trained to heal people - not kill them," Andy was saying. "Look - even if they do find out - Aiden was an accident. Right? That's what you said. He fell and hit his head. He attacked you, so you pushed him. It was self defense."

"It's too late," said the other voice. "Who's going to buy that, after all these ...."

The conversation was interrupted by barking. Furious barking. Suddenly, Jane saw the classroom light come on through the crack under the door. Somebody had come. Should she yell? She held her breath. What if it was an accomplice?

"Jane? You in here?" called a woman's voice. It was Pam.

Jane started to answer, but stopped herself. If she yelled, would she put Pam in danger?

"Oh, Andy, it's you," Pam said. "Hi. But what are you ...? Hey, Sam. Did Cathy go home? You'll have to tell her that the concert was wonderful."

Tillie started barking.

"Tillie, no," Pam said. "Sit. That's a good girl. You guys wouldn't happen to have seen Jane, would you? Tillie about went crazy outside. Nearly pulled my arm off, trying to get in here. I thought maybe she smelled Jane. See, she was coming to get Betsy's pan. But Betsy just texted me. Jane was supposed to bring it over to her house, but she never showed up. And I remembered that I moved all my stuff into the cubbies in the hallway - in case somebody locked the classroom. I tried to text Jane to tell her, but she didn't answer. So, I thought I'd better come over and check. Her car's still out front. I'm afraid she's gotten herself tangled up in those crutches and fallen."

"Sorry," Andy said. "We only just got here. We haven't...."

All of a sudden, the ringtone on Jane's phone - the minuet - began to play. The sound was coming from somewhere in the classroom.

"That's her phone!" Pam exclaimed. "She must be around here somewhere. Jane! Jane, where are you?"

Tillie started barking again. From the closet, Jane could see the dog's big paws scrabbling under the closet door. Jane's head was pounding. Should she call out? Would she be putting Pam in danger?

"Tillie, what are you doing under there?" Pam said. "What's this table doing here? Why's it blocking the closet?"

Jane heard something heavy being slid across the floor. She heard Pam exclaim: "Oh, my God! These are Jane's crutches! Where is she? Jane!"

As the closet door burst open, Jane scrabbled to her feet. Pain streaked up her leg, but she held onto the hammer that she'd taken from the closet shelf. With her free hand, she grabbed Pam's arm and pulled her into the closet to get her away from the men. "Dial 9-1-1!" Jane screamed. "Pam, quick!"

The classroom exploded into a clamor of noise and motion. Tillie bolted to the door, barking, as Beau Strickland and a uniformed policeman rushed in, two paramedics behind them. With the doorway blocked, Andy and Sam were trapped.

Jane pointed at them. "They're the ones," she said. "They killed Aiden!" As Beau stepped toward the men, the other policeman pulled out his gun. And Tillie rushed into the closet, leaped onto Jane, and began swabbing her cheek and ear.

CHAPTER TWENTY-FIVE

"So, the police and the ambulance arrived at the same time?" Grace asked. "How'd you manage to send for both, Pam?"

"I didn't," Pam said. "They didn't respond to my call."

"What do you mean?" Grace asked. "You just said you dialed 9-1-1. And the police and ambulance arrived. I'm confused."

Betsy came in from the kitchen, holding two ice packs. "They were responding to my call, not Pam's," she explained. "I'd already dialed 9-1-1. Pam called them, but I called them first. They were already on the way." Betsy handed two ice packs to Jane, who was sitting on the couch, with her injured leg on the ottoman and an afghan wrapped around her shoulders. Jane put one ice pack on her head and the other on her ankle, then handed Betsy the melting packs that she'd been using. She shut her eyes, content to let her friends piece together the details of the horrible night without her help.

Ruth Alice and the rest of Jane's watercolor group had been dribbling in throughout the morning. Betsy had greeted them at the door, so Jane wouldn't have to get up. Since Jane had a concussion, the medics told her she needed to rest. And they didn't want her staying by herself, so Betsy had spent the night. She'd been watching over Jane like a mother hen.

Each of the painters arrived laden with food, as well as concern about Jane's health and curiosity about what had happened. As each one arrived, Betsy and Pam had to recount the story: How it had started with Betsy's lasagna pan. After the gala, Jane had offered to take it to Betsy's house. But when Jane didn't show up, Betsy had gotten worried and texted Pam. Pam was helping Chandler remove the lights from the golf cart, and, at first, she missed seeing the text. As soon as she did notice it, she went up to the Studio Annex in search of Jane. Tillie had practically broken the door to get inside the building, and that made Pam suspicious that something was amiss. She'd come upon Andy Harrison and Sam Barron in the darkened classroom, and that struck her as odd. Then, when Jane's phone started ringing in the classroom, Pam knew something was wrong. As soon as she saw Jane's crutches under the table, she was sure that Jane was hurt, so she pressed 9-1-1 on her phone.

"I've finally learned to take my phone with me," Pam said. "Unlike that time when Jane and I were in the bomb shelter - when the wall collapsed."

Maisie didn't arrive until it was nearly lunchtime, and she was still trying to piece together the details while Betsy was in the kitchen assembling sandwiches. How Jane had gotten the concussion. Why the police had taken Andy Harrison and Sam Barron in handcuffs to jail. What all of this had to do with the murder of Aiden Parson.

"I still don't get it," Maisie called to Betsy in the kitchen. "You were at home, Betsy. So, how did you know to call 9-1-1?'

"When Jane didn't show up at my house, I knew something was wrong," Betsy said. Wiping her hands on an apron, Betsy came to the doorway and switched into her calm, ever-patient, occupational therapist voice. She ran through the timeline, again: "So, I texted Pam. She texted back that Jane had probably gone over to the Studio Annex to get my lasagna pan. I knew Jane couldn't walk on the grass with crutches, so that meant she would've been all alone on that dark road, with cars going by. I was afraid she'd fallen. Or worse, gotten hit. I was going to wake up Jim and go look for her. Then, I got to thinking that even if she was in the building, she would have been alone on a deserted campus. Anything could have happened. So I decided to call 9-1-1 and request both a medical and a police unit. I figured it was probably a false alarm, but better safe than sorry."

Ruth Alice waited until Betsy brought Maisie up to speed. Then she looked at Jane. "Do you really think they would have killed you?" Ruth

Alice asked. "I mean, Andy's a medical doctor. And they both know you. You're friends with Sam's wife, aren't you?"

"I don't know what they would've done," Jane said. "I really don't." She felt a tear spring out of one eye and roll down her cheek. She realized that she was exhausted, inside and out.

Grace brought over a box of tissues and sat down on the couch beside Jane. She put her arm around Jane's shoulder.

"I'm sorry. I know I'm a total wreck," Jane said. "Between my head aching and my ankle throbbing, I couldn't sleep. I kept playing the whole thing over and over in my head. I remember standing in the art closet, looking at Tony's painting. After I turned it over and realized there was a painting on the other side, I took it out of the closet to get a better look. I don't know what happened next. The lights went out. Literally. The next thing I knew, I was in the closet on that freezing floor, and those men were talking about killing me." Jane shivered.

"Maybe we better talk about something else," Grace announced. "This is too much for you."

Jane frowned. "No, I think it's better to talk through it. Make sense of it. Maybe it will help me process it." She looked at the comforting, sympathetic faces surrounding her in her sunny living room. "You know, I'm pretty sure Andy Harrison didn't want to kill me. He was trying to talk Sam into calling the police."

"They must have known that once they called the police," Ruth Alice said, "it was all over. They'd have to confess to the art forgeries. And Aiden's death."

Jane sighed. "When I was listening from the closet, Andy said they could claim that I'd been mugged. That they were the ones who'd found me and come to my rescue. But I don't think Sam was going to go along with it. The way he was talking - he wanted Andy to make it look like a medical thing. Like I had an aneurysm and died."

"You know, I doubt if Aiden's death was really an accident," Maisie said. "That's what Sam might be claiming. And maybe Andy believed him, at the time. But it really sounds like Sam Barron is capable of murder."

"All that stuff he was saying when I was in the closet - about making me disappear," Jane said, "won't help his defense. That's for sure."

"Poor Jane," Grace said. "All you went through! You must have been terrified. And poor Cathy Barron. Can you imagine being married to a man like Sam?"

"So, you're saying that when the police arrived, Sam and Andy confessed. They told the police that Aiden's death was an accident, " Maisie said. "According to them, Sam was in the old cemetery with Aiden, and the two of them got into a shoving match. Aiden fell and hit his head. But where was Andy? He wasn't with them at the time?"

Jane shrugged. "Apparently not."

"Why the cemetery?" Maisie asked. "What did that have to do with it?"

"It was where they kept the art. The wall in the old bomb shelter had started to cave in. Aiden discovered it." Jane said. "The dirt under the lowest shelf was crumbling, and Aiden realized there was an old cemetery abutting the bomb shelter. He knew it was a perfect place to hide the forged paintings. Whenever they got a shipment of forged art, Aiden would fit the paintings into frames. Then they'd store the art in the cemetery until the dealer found buyers."

"So they kept tampering with the wall. Digging it out and then packing it back together? That must be why it collapsed - because it got weakened," said Maisie. She looked at Pam. "Not because you sneezed."

"But I do have powerful sneezes," Pam said.

"Who supplied the forged paintings?" Maisie asked.

"That shady art dealer - the one who sold the fake Bierstadt to the Gulch Museum," Jane said. "Evidently, Aiden continued his relationship with that dealer after he came to Atkinsville."

"But how did Sam Barron get involved?" Maisie asked.

"He gets shipments of antiques for his store," Jane said. "Aiden didn't paint the forgeries himself, but he knew how to recognize and restore old frames. At some point, Sam must have figured out what Aiden was up to - buying all those frames - and they went into business together."

"But Andy Harrison is a doctor," Maisie said. "What did he have to do with it?"

"I remember he had that painting in his office," Grace said. She looked at Jane. "Remember? With the fancy frame. He seemed to know a lot about old frames."

Jane nodded. "He said he'd wanted to go to art school," Jane said. "Remember, he told us that? But his father and grandfather urged him to go to medical school, instead. It's sort of ironic. He told us he became a doctor because he'd make more money."

"I still don't understand," Maisie said. "Why would he get involved in art forgery?"

"Money. He was desperate for money," Jane said. "He had a gambling problem. When they were handcuffing him, Andy broke down and started sobbing. Said his family was bankrupt because of him. He'd ruined their name. Because of his gambling addiction, they had to sell off the family estate."

"That must have been tough," Grace said. "The Harrisons have owned that land for generations."

"So, those three - Aiden, Sam Barron, and Andy Harrison - were all involved in this art forgery ring?" Ruth Alice said. "And they ran it out of AAC. Now, that's fairly alarming."

Jane looked at Ruth Alice. She felt the glimmer of a smile forming - her first smile in what seemed like ages. "I believe your next line is: 'Never a dull moment.'"

Ruth Alice chuckled. "I believe you're right."

"But I still don't understand what Tony Keller's painting has to do with it," Maisie said.

"His painting was in a really fancy frame," Jane explained. "It was heavy, and it looked old. That's the kind of frame that Aiden and Sam were looking for. But Tony saw that one first, and he grabbed it."

"You're saying they didn't care about Tony's painting?" Maisie said. "Just the frame?"

"Well, that's the amazing thing," Jane said. "They just lucked into a really valuable painting. It was in one of the shipments. The painting was an Old Master. Not a forgery. It was done on a wood panel - not a canvas. Aiden recognized it. He rubbed the dirt off to expose the signature. That's what Sam was afraid that I'd notice. That's when he knocked me off my feet."

"Were you able to read the signature?" Ruth Alice asked. "Who was the painter?"

"Calame," Jane said. She spelled out the letters. "Have you ever heard of him?"

Ruth Alice nodded. "Yes. He was Swiss. Alexandre Calame. He did landscapes. Middle of the nineteenth century. Sometimes there were little figures in the landscapes. He's not well known outside the art world, but recently one of his paintings brought millions at auction. It made the news."

"So, you're saying that while they were looking for old frames to use with forgeries, they happened upon a genuine Old Master?" Maisie said. "That's ironic."

"It is," Jane said. "I guess they figured they'd uncovered a goldmine. A real Old Master. They could refurbish it and auction it off. But Tony Keller had fallen in love with the frame, and he refused to give it up. Sam didn't want to make a big deal of it, because he didn't want Tony to get suspicious. They figured Tony would pop out the wood panel with what he assumed was a worthless, damaged, old painting on it. But instead of tossing it in the dumpster - like they thought he would - Tony painted his own picture on the reverse side of it. So, Aiden made sure that Tony's painting was accepted into the Summerfest Exhibit. They thought they could buy it and recover the Old Master. But Tony marked it, 'not for sale.' That gave them no choice but to steal it."

"And they hid the painting in the old cemetery," Maisie said.

Jane nodded.

"And Sam and Aiden got into a fight?" Ruth Alice asked. "And Aiden was killed."

"Yes."

"Why'd they leave his body in the cemetery?" Maisie asked.

Jane shrugged. "A cemetery is the perfect place to hide a dead body, isn't it? Sam opened one of the caskets, pulled out the bones, and put Aiden's body in."

"But you found the skeleton in the art closet," Maisie said.

"That's right. Sam put the bones in there. Along with the painting," Jane said.

"Why didn't he leave the skeleton in the cemetery?" Maisie said.

"I don't know," Jane said. "I think he panicked when he realized Aiden was dead. He walled up the cemetery as fast as he could. Then he realized that he had incriminating evidence - the child's skeleton and Tony's painting. What better place to hide a skeleton than in an art closet - where they store skeletons for students to draw?"

"And what better place to hide a painting than in an art closet?" Ruth Alice said. "Where stacks of student paintings are stored."

"Then that kid started screaming about the skeleton at the Halloween reception," Betsy said, as she marched out of the kitchen, carrying a tray of sandwiches. "And when we put Old Yorick back in the closet, we discovered the real skeleton - the bones of the child from the cemetery - in there."

"That was a coincidence, wasn't it," Grace said. "That they put the skeleton in the closet during the reception."

"Not really," Jane said. "Whenever there's an event at AAC, lots of people are coming and going. Getting supplies out of the closet. Walking through the tunnel. That would be the best time to deposit a skeleton, a painting - whatever - in the closet."

"What I don't understand is why the painting was on the floor after the gala," Grace said. "Where you almost tripped over it."

"I bet I know," Ruth Alice said. "After the gala, AAC closes for the holidays. The buildings are deserted. But nobody would notice activity on the night of the gala. Volunteers are cleaning up, packing away decorations. So, that would be a perfect time to go into the classroom and get the painting. Jane must have surprised Sam when she entered the building. He put the painting down and hid."

The doorbell rang. Grace went to get it.

Donna was standing on the front porch, holding a large bouquet.

"Well, isn't that nice of you!" Grace exclaimed at the door. "Look, everyone! Donna brought flowers for Jane. They're beautiful. Purple roses and heart-shaped anthuriums. Very striking."

"Don't get all gracious, Grace," Donna said as she came into the living room. "They aren't from me. They were on the steps when Bill dropped me off." She untied the bow surrounding the vase of flowers and handed Jane an envelope attached to the ribbon. The envelope was bulging. "It's addressed to Shirley Holmes."

Jane opened the envelope and removed a dog biscuit and a card. "It's from Beau Strickland," she announced. "He says this is the closest he could get to issuing me a purple heart for bravery in the line of duty. 'Congratulations,' he says, 'for cracking your second murder investigation. The biscuit is for your canine assistant.'"

Jane looked up, grinning. "And in parenthesis, he added that if I find any other skeletons in the art closet, would I please leave them there."

Book Club Discussion Suggestions for
SKELETON IN THE ART CLOSET

Plot

- Mysteries always include misleading clues and "red herrings." What were the misleading clues in this story? Did you guess whodunnit before the end? If so, how did you figure it out?
- How did the author's research help her develop the plot and characters? Although this is a work of fiction, she researched various topics - tonsillectomies, forensics, Fragile X syndrome, Western art, art forgery. Did anything in the story prompt you to go online to find out more information?
- How did the author's experience as a painter and a volunteer at an art center contribute to the story?
- Many readers enjoy mystery stories. In your opinion, what makes these stories compelling? Why do you enjoy reading mysteries?

Characters

- Which of the characters did you relate to? If you had to pick one of these characters to be your painting companion, who would you choose? Who was your favorite character, and why? Which character resembles you the most?
- Jane and her friends belong to a painting group that meets weekly. Do you belong to any groups that meet regularly? Do the interactions between members of your group remind you of the interactions between members of Jane's watercolor painting group? In what way?
- Friends offer a mirror by which we can see ourselves more clearly. What does Jane learn about herself during the various interactions with her painting companions? What have you learned about yourself by interacting with groups?
- All of the painters in Jane's watercolor group are women. How would the group's interactions change if men were members?

ACKNOWLEDGEMENTS

Writing is mostly a solo journey, so I'm grateful to our amazing local arts center, OCAF (Oconee Cultural Arts Foundation) in Watkinsville Georgia, where I find inspiration, enthusiasm, and companionship. Special thanks to my writing group for abetting my career in crime: Debra Harden, Muriel Pritchett, and Susan Vizurraga. And thanks to the Women of Watercolor, who inspire my prose as well as my paintings: Patricia A. Adams, Loretta Hammer, Diane Norman Powelson, Janet Rodekohr, Barbara Schell, and Mia York.

Home is my haven for cozy writing and colorful painting. Thanks to my understanding husband, Chester Karwoski, for nurturing me. Thanks to my wonderful daughters, Leslie Anderson and Geneva Karwoski for encouraging mom's latest projects. Thanks to my extraordinary son-in-laws, Lucas Anderson and Andy Gassaway, for welcoming me into your homes for restorative respites from writing. And thanks to my favorite little readers, Clementine, Lola, Prairie, and Augie, who remind me that words and stories are a lifelong source of fun.

ABOUT THE AUTHOR

Gail Langer Karwoski is the author of *A Brush with Murder*, the first cozy in the Black Rose Writing *Watercolor Mystery* series. She has also written *The Wedding Heard 'Round the World; America's First Gay Marriage* and 14 books for young readers. Her award-winning juvenile novels include *Seaman, the Dog Who Explored the West with Lewis and Clark* and *Quake! Disaster in San Francisco, 1906*. Gail also wrote the acclaimed bedtime story, *Water Beds, Sleeping in the Ocean*. When Gail isn't at her keyboard, you can find her painting with watercolors. Or cuddling her cat while she reads cozy mysteries.

NOTE FROM THE AUTHOR

Word-of-mouth is crucial for any author to succeed. If you enjoyed *Skeleton in the Art Closet*, please leave a review online—anywhere you are able. Even if it's just a sentence or two. It would make all the difference and would be very much appreciated.

Thanks!
Gail Langer Karwoski

We hope you enjoyed reading this title from:

BLACK ❀ ROSE
writing™

www.blackrosewriting.com

Subscribe to our mailing list – *The Rosevine* – and receive **FREE** books, daily
deals, and stay current with news about upcoming
releases and our hottest authors.
Scan the QR code below to sign up.

Already a subscriber? Please accept a sincere thank you for being a fan of
Black Rose Writing authors.

View other Black Rose Writing titles at
www.blackrosewriting.com/books and use promo code
PRINT to receive a **20% discount** when purchasing.

CPSIA information can be obtained
at www.ICGtesting.com
Printed in the USA
JSHW031037170323
39062JS00003B/13